Wild Horse River

Wild Horse River

Wayne D. Overholser

THORNDIKE
CHIVERS

This Large Print edition is published by Thorndike Press®, Waterville, Maine USA and by BBC Audiobooks, Ltd, Bath, England.

Published in 2004 in the U.S. by arrangement with Golden West Literary Agency.

Published in 2004 in the U.K. by arrangement with Golden West Literary Agency.

U.S. Hardcover   0-7862-6922-7 (Western)
U.K. Hardcover   1-4056-3131-7 (Chivers Large Print)
U.K. Softcover   1-4056-3132-5 (Camden Large Print)

The text of this Large Print edition is unabridged.
Other aspects of the book may vary from the original edition.

Set in 16 pt. Plantin by Al Chase.

Printed in the United States on permanent paper.

British Library Cataloguing-in-Publication Data available

Library of Congress Cataloging-in-Publication Data

Overholser, Wayne D., 1906–
  Wild horse river : a western story / Wayne D. Overholser.
    p. cm.
  ISBN 0-7862-6922-7 (lg. print : hc : alk. paper)
    1. Sheriffs — Fiction.   2. Ranchers — Fiction.   3. Large type books.   I. Title.
  PS3529.V33W55 2004
  813'.54—dc22   2004053713

Wild Horse River

Chapter One

By nature, Jim Bruce was neither a dreamer nor an idealist. He was a cowman, as indigenous of the country as the grass itself, a tall, lean-bodied man with the bowlegs and long bones of one who has been physically shaped by countless hours in the saddle, a practical man who understood the uses of branding iron and rope and gun as tools of the trade in which he was trained. Yet, paradoxically, he had become a dreamer, an idealist, and the sheriff of San Marcos County, all within the year.

Now, near evening in late summer, he rode down San Marcos Creek, leaving the good grass behind him that was K Cross winter range, inwardly a little sour because it had been a wasted day. Holt Klein, the K Cross owner, had claimed for months that he was losing beef, yet now, as several times before, a careful search along the creek had not turned up any proof that stolen cattle had crossed the stream.

There was a grim sort of humor in this business of Jim Bruce trying to find out who was stealing Klein's beef. He had not been

7

the big cowman's choice for sheriff. It had been the wild bunch on Banjo Mesa, the townsmen in Harmony, and the small ranchers on the desert east of the creek who had banded together to elect him.

Klein had started talking about losing cattle shortly after election, and he had made his brag that, if Jim didn't stop it, he'd personally run every tough hand off Banjo Mesa — and he'd clear the desert of the ten-cow ranchers. If Jim couldn't handle his job, Klein would see to it that a man got the star that could.

Reaching the Ryan cabin, Jim pulled his roan gelding to a stop and sat there, letting the memories torture him. The Ryans had been his neighbors for a long time, and then two years ago it had happened: Tim Ryan had been dry-gulched. His horses and cattle had disappeared. Lizzie Ryan, Tim's wife, had died from a heart attack. The girl Molly had moved into Harmony and was now working in the hotel, swearing that she'd save her money, and, when she had enough to buy a herd and hire a crew, she'd come back.

Funny, Jim thought, *how nature changes a girl when she grows up.* Molly was five years younger than Jim. He remembered her as a freckle-faced kid with the disposition of an

8

imp and a right arm that could throw a snowball harder and straighter than any boy on the creek. She still had the freckles and the easy smile she'd had as a child, but she'd changed into a mature and pretty woman who had half the single men in the county in love with her.

Jim rolled a smoke, his eyes on the cabin with its broken windows and the door sagging from one hinge. The windmill tower had blown down, the corrals needed repairing, and weeds had grown up in the yard. To Jim, there was nothing more pathetic than a deserted ranch, especially this one where he had been almost as much at home as he had on Pitchfork, his own place a mile down the creek.

The sun was half hidden behind the tall, gaunt peaks of the Ramparts west of Wild Horse River. Shadows had gathered in the cedars and piñons covering Banjo Mesa that lay between the river and the Ramparts, but the valley was still touched by the light of the dying sun. Far to the east, across the desert, the San Juan range was bright with the sunset. In a few minutes that, too, would be gone.

There had always been something mysterious and a little weird about a sunset to Jim. Even as a boy he had felt it, perhaps because his mother had feared the darkness. It was the devil's time, she said, when he could work without being seen. Daylight belonged to the Lord. She had been afraid of storms, too. When they had blown up over the Ramparts and lightning had fried the sky and thunder had boomed like the roar of bigmouthed cannon, his mother would say the Lord and the devil were fighting for the souls of men.

Jim didn't know much about what happened to the souls of men, but as far as he was concerned, the devil was Holt Klein. If he lived to be a million years old, he would never forget how Lizzie Ryan had looked the morning he'd brought in Tim's body. It was as if she had decided that minute to die so that she could be with her husband. She had, a few months later.

Jim crushed out his cigarette and turned his gelding down the creek. Molly never came out here. She said there wasn't any use breaking her heart over something she couldn't do anything about, but it was different with Jim. He usually spent a couple of nights a week at Pitchfork, leaving his young deputy, Dobe Jackson, to handle the trivial problems that took much of a sheriff's time. Dobe always knew where to find him if an emergency came up.

Jim's folks had died several years before the Ryans had, but he would have made out by himself if the bank had not pressed him for the money he owed. He had sold off his cattle to keep the bank off his neck, hanging on to a few horses and the section of land his father had owned here in the triangle formed by San Marcos Creek and the river. After that he'd run for sheriff, hoping to save enough out of his salary to restock his range.

It was nearly dark when he reached Pitchfork, and he rode on down to the river and watered his horse. He stood there for a time, the reins in his hand, listening to the roar of the water in the gorge above him.

At this point, Wild Horse River rolled by as smooth and black as chipped obsidian, but in the gorge to the west it was a white frothing torrent, tumbling around huge boulders and pressed in between the sandstone walls that rose a sheer five hundred feet on both sides.

There was no record of anyone ever having run the gorge and lived, although several had tried. Even as a boy, Jim had felt the challenge of the river, but it was a challenge he had never accepted, mostly because he saw little sense in risking his life for no purpose except to prove he could do something that had never been done.

Jim led his horse to the corral and unsaddled, feeling the pull of the river more than he ever had before. Old Bill Gray, who operated a sort of tollgate at the ford above the gorge, owned a boat, and Jim found himself wondering if he could buy it. It was a crazy notion, and he put it out of his mind. If he wanted to die, it had better be with a gun in his hand facing Holt Klein.

He walked to his cabin, listening to the siren beat of the river, and then he stopped, startled. In the thin light he saw that the front door of his cabin was open. The discovery shocked him, his mind gripping the thought that death might be waiting here for him. He was certain that he had closed the door the last time he had been here. As he stepped up on the porch, a board squeaked under foot, shrill and loud in the darkness; he felt heat flow out of the cabin and he smelled coffee.

For a moment Jim doubted his sanity. He'd been thinking of the past too much, of his folks and the Ryans and the river. If one of his friends were here, there would be a light. He stood at the edge of the doorway and drew his gun, a chill traveling down his spine.

The interior of the room was pitch black

except for the faint glow of fire in the range. He lunged through the door and put his back to the wall, the pound of his heels on the floor beneath hitting his ears with pistol sharpness.

Someone yawned, and a woman asked: "That you, Jim?"

He stood there a moment, laboring for breath as he tried to identify the voice. It was familiar, but not familiar enough for him to place the speaker. He was certain it wasn't Molly, and he didn't know any other woman who would come here.

"Make yourself known!" the woman cried, frightened now. "If you aren't Jim Bruce, I'm going to start shooting."

"It's me," Jim said.

The woman took a sighing breath of relief. "You were a long time saying so. You gave me a turn."

He heard her cross the room to the table. She struck a match and lighted a lamp, and, when she turned to face him, he saw that it was Angela Klein, Holt Klein's wife. She sat down, trembling, her face white.

"I've had supper ready for a long time," she said, "but I've got to get over the shakes before I put it on the table. Holt said you were up the creek trying to cut sign on the rustlers, so I knew you'd stop here on your way into town."

He realized that his gun was still in his hand. He holstered it, feeling a little foolish and not knowing what to say. "Sorry I scared you. Didn't expect to find anyone here."

She laughed shakily. "I should have lighted the lamp. Maybe I scared you a little."

"Sort of."

She rose. "I thought you'd be here before dark, but I got tired, waiting, and laid down. I didn't intend to go to sleep."

She turned to the stove and started taking biscuits out of a pan. He watched her, suspicious of her but not sure whether he had a right to be. She was much younger than Klein, not quite thirty, although she had been married to him for twelve years.

Jim had never known her well. She had come from a raggle-taggle desert family that had somehow eked out a living east of the creek. He remembered that she had been pretty as a girl, even in the faded calico dresses that poverty had forced her to wear. Now she was beautiful, although Klein seemed to find no pride in her beauty. She seldom left K Cross, and it was even more seldom that she came to town. For her to be here alone was unreasonable.

"Holt's pretty worried about his losses," Angela said. "I guess you know that. The trouble with Holt is that he doesn't know how people feel, but I do. Anything that can be stolen from his outfit is fair game, and maybe it is when you think of the things he's done."

She had the table set. Now she poured coffee and put the biscuits and bacon on the table. She drew chairs up and turned to look at him, smiling. Her features were perfect; her yellow hair was pinned in a sort of crown on top of her head. She stood close to the table, her green eyes bright in the lamplight.

"Look, Sheriff," she said. "I've waited two hours to eat with you and these biscuits are as hard as rocks. The bacon's greasy and the coffee's strong enough to walk out of here if I gave it a push. Now, are you going to keep on standing there, or are you going to sit down?"

"Sure," he said, and hung his hat on a nail.

He walked across the room, found that the water bucket on the bench was half full, and poured some into the wash pan. As he washed, he tried to think of a reason for Angela's presence, and failed. It was no secret that she did not love her husband, although it might have been to Klein, who never seemed to be aware of anyone's feelings but his own. Too, there was gossip that Angela was having an affair with the K Cross foreman, Sam Pruett, but gossip-mongers were no different on Wild Horse range than anywhere else, and Jim had always discounted the stories.

He sat down at the table, uneasiness growing in him, but if Angela sensed his feelings, she gave no indication of it. As she had said, the biscuits were hard, the coffee strong, but Jim was too hungry to notice. He kept his eyes on the plate, and, even when Angela rose to fill his coffee cup, he did not look at her.

Finished, he leaned back and rolled a smoke, forcing himself to ask the question that must be asked sooner or later. "Why did you come here, Missus Klein?"

"I'm Angela to my friends," she said quickly. "Or maybe I'm not a friend. Is that what you're trying to say, Jim?"

She rose and cleared the table. He was silent for a time, thinking again of the poverty she'd known as a girl. Klein was niggardly with her, or so the talk went, but still the brown riding skirt and the tan shirt-waist were not much like the drab dresses she had worn before she was married.

"No," he said. "I don't blame you for what Holt's done."

"Thank you," she said simply. "Remember one thing, Jim. I've been married for twelve years. That's a big piece of time to take out of a person's life." She turned her back to him and began washing dishes. "When I was seventeen, I thought that any marriage would be a good one, but I was never more wrong about anything."

She was silent for a long time. Jim finished his cigarette and, walking to the door, tossed the stub into the yard. A storm was building up over the Ramparts. He could see lightning working among the granite peaks and he heard the distant thunder. He thought of his mother's fear of storms and her notion that they were the battlefields on which the Lord and the devil fought for the souls of men, and he found himself wondering what Angela would think if he told her about it.

When Angela finished the dishes, she crossed the room to him and stood behind him. She asked, her tone low: "Are you in love, Jim?"

"No."

"Turn around, Jim. I want to see your face."

He made the turn, saying: "Maybe we'd

better ride into town."

She smiled. "There's no hurry, is there, Jim? Or are you afraid of what Holt will do?"

"No."

"Then you're afraid of what people will say, about you and me."

"No, damn it. I'm not afraid."

She stood quite close to him, her face up-turned. He was aware of the pulse beat in her throat, of the rise and fall of her firm round breasts. He was stirred by her near-ness as any man would have been stirred, but he had lied to her when he'd said he was not afraid. If she had been any other woman, it might have been different, but she was Holt Klein's wife, and that fact could not be changed no matter how she felt toward him. Yet it was not entirely a lie. He was not afraid of Klein or what people would say. He was afraid of her.

"I know what you think of Holt," she said, "and you have every right to think it. When I married him, K Cross was a little outfit just like the rest of them. It's since then that he's grown fat on the bones of other men. He's killed and he's robbed and he's threat-ened. He's used every weapon he could to reach the place that he has, and still he isn't satisfied."

It was true. Jim knew it was true, and

18

Molly Ryan knew it was true, but knowing it and doing something about it were two different things. He said slowly: "If you can prove he's killed a man, any particular man, like Tim Ryan, I'll arrest him and he'll stand trial."

She smiled, a small, bitter curve of her lips. "You're talking crazy, Jim. In the first place, I can't prove it. Not the way I'd have to in court. In the second place, I couldn't testify against him."

"Then why are you saying this?"

"Because I like you," she said simply, "and because I've spent a lot of time at night, when I couldn't sleep, thinking how different my life would have been if I had married a man like you. We all want happiness, Jim. It's what we're alive for, I guess. Well, I've never known an hour of happiness from the day I married Holt."

She stood there within reach of his arms, waiting for him to put them around her, throwing herself at him in a way no other woman had ever done. Still he kept his arms at his sides. There was something back of it he could not understand, something she wanted from him.

"I'm sorry," he said.

"Sorry." The bitter smile touched her lips again. "A poor word, Jim. I think you're in love with someone else. With Molly Ryan, maybe."

"No."

"Or Linda Gale."

He frowned, thinking of Linda Gale, who lived on Banjo Mesa. They were a strange clannish lot, the mesa people, marrying among themselves and holding a tight, hostile front toward anyone from the outside.

Perhaps he did love Linda, although he had never thought of it in quite that way. He had admired her from the first moment he had met her, and he had often wished there was some way to get her off the mesa so she could live like a civilized person, but he had done nothing more than wish. A man couldn't court a woman when she showed no interest in him.

There was no use telling Angela how he felt about Linda, so he said again: "No."

"You were slow denying it," Angela said. "But if you love her, you're wasting it on a woman you'll never have."

"I know." He watched bitterness mar her features and leave its ugliness there, and he asked sharply: "What do you want of me?"

"Your friendship," she answered. "Call it love if you want to. I hoped that I would leave here tonight feeling that there was one man on this range who thinks kindly of me."

"You're after something else," he said bluntly. "Why don't you say it?"

She turned away. "All right. I'm after something else, but I won't tell you what it is, because you're afraid of Holt just like the others. Someday I'll kill him, I suppose, and you'll arrest me. You'll call it a duty, just like it's my duty to be loyal to him because I made the mistake of marrying him."

She picked up a lantern and handed it to him. He took it, wondering if he was making a mistake. He could not be certain, but he had a feeling that Angela knew enough of her husband's actions to hang him. He watched her blow out the lamp, and for a moment he remained in the doorway, the blackness hiding her. Then he jacked up the chimney and lighted the lantern. They left the cabin together, Jim pulling the door shut.

She said nothing more until he saddled her horse. She mounted, and then she said: "I've failed, Jim. I should have known. I made the mistake of being direct, and that never works with a man."

He threw gear on his roan gelding, not knowing what to say to her, then he blew out the lantern and left it inside the barn. He stepped into the saddle and they turned toward town.

"I think you'll come to me, Jim," she went on, "although it may be too late. You'll never forget tonight and you'll keep wondering about the mistake you've just made. Together, we could lick Holt. But you're afraid, Jim. Somehow I got the notion that you were one man who was not afraid of Holt."

"I'm not," he said sharply. "Not like you're making out, but there's some things that are decent and some that ain't."

"So I'm not decent."

"I didn't say that."

There was no sound then except the roar of the river muted by the walls of the gorge and the soft *thud* of hoofs in the deep dust of the road. Presently the lights of Harmony showed ahead.

This was something he could see through. She thought she could prod him into killing Holt Klein by this talk of his being afraid. He said sharply: "I may kill Klein, but I won't start gunning for him because you're trying to hooraw me into it."

"Then he'll kill you. I'm not trying to hooraw you into anything. I'm trying to save you, but you're either not smart enough to see that, or you're too proud. I'll tell you something, Jim. The only setback Holt has had since I married him was when you were elected, and he means to get you out of office in one way or another."

"I can believe that."

"Then can't you see you need me?"

"No."

She took a long breath, and he thought she was close to crying. "Jim, Jim, I thought my loving you was enough, but I see I was wrong. I'll go on hoping you will come to me sometime before it's too late."

They had reached the town now and he said: "I'll go with you to the hotel and put your horse away."

"No!" she cried, frightened now. "I don't want Holt to know who I was with. I'll go in alone."

She touched her horse up and rode on toward the business block, the lamps in the saloons and hotel throwing splashes of yellow light across the dull red dust of the street. He let her go, relieved to be rid of her, and turned into an alley behind the house he rented.

He put his horse away and went inside. For a time, he sat in his front room, smoking and thinking about Angela. It was like a crazy dream that might well have been a nightmare if he had yielded to the desire she had aroused in him. She hardly knew him. He had talked to her more tonight than he had since she'd been married. Before that he had just been a neighbor kid on the other side of the creek from the desert place where her folks lived. The difference now was that he was sheriff, and it was probably the reason she had come to him.

Some of the things she had said were lies. She didn't love him. If she thought she did, she was crazy. But some of the things she had said were true. Klein would not rest until he had put his man into office. Perhaps this was his way of going at it. But that didn't seem right, either. Thinking about it now in the darkness, he felt sure that Angela was telling the truth when she had hinted at wanting to see Holt Klein dead.

Jim went to bed, wondering if Klein had been losing stock, or whether it was his way of stirring up trouble for Jim. Certainly there was no evidence of it along the creek. That left Gray's Crossing. It was possible that the mesa men, and that included Linda Gale's brothers, were stealing K Cross beef. If they were, they would have to bring the cattle across the river at Gray's Crossing. Jim's deputy, young Dobe Jackson, was up there now, watching.

Jim would see Dobe in the morning, and he'd talk to old man Gray. Then he shook his head, staring at the dark ceiling. Gray

24

was close-mouthed, and he had to keep on good terms with the mesa people. It was not likely the old man would say anything, but there was a chance Dobe had picked something up.

Chapter Two

It was daylight when Jim awoke. He got up and dressed, feeling as tired as when he had gone to bed. Usually he cooked his own meals, but this morning he decided to invest in a hotel breakfast. It wasn't that he didn't want to bother. He had to see Molly. Hearing her laugh and swapping words with her was enough to lift a man's spirits — and Jim needed his spirits lifted. He was alone too much.

There were times when he wondered if he had any friends in San Marcos County except Dobe Jackson and Molly. And Doc Foster. Certainly he could not number all the men who had voted for him among his friends. It had been their way of striking at Holt Klein.

Now, after a year in office, some of them were wondering if he had sold out to Klein. It was a natural suspicion, hating and fearing Klein as most of them did. To their way of thinking, it shouldn't take Jim a year to get enough evidence on Klein to throw him into jail.

He buckled his gun belt around him and

stepped into the street. This was late summer, and it was warm, even at seven o'clock in the morning. By noon it would be hot, typical western Colorado heat that dried a man's sweat the instant it broke through his skin. Jim moved down the street, raising his eyes enviously to the Ramparts that made a long spiny crest to the north and west of town.

The mountains formed a definite barrier between Utah and Colorado, penetrated, or so the rumor went, only by the hardy outlaws who made it to Wild Horse River one jump ahead of a posse and threaded the Ramparts by way of passes known only to members of their dark trail brotherhood. It was one of the points Holt Klein always made when he talked about running everybody off Banjo Mesa. He was mighty damned tired, he'd say, of having San Marcos County known as an outlaw hangout.

It was something else for which Jim had no proof, for he'd never had positive knowledge that an outlaw had escaped Colorado law by working his way through the Ramparts, or that any of them had been guided to safety by the mesa people, as Klein made out. But this morning Jim refused to think about outlaws. His mind was on the more pleasant subject of trout that grew big in the deep pools of the river above the gorge. Then he shrugged. Trout fishing wasn't for him. Not with Holt Klein threatening to clear the mesa of every settler who roosted there.

Jim moved along the boardwalk toward the hotel, hearing the growl of the river as it whipped through the gorge. He looked southward at the Red Wall that lay on the other side of the river, marking Banjo Mesa's southern edge. It lay in a half circle, a great sandstone cliff with a slick-rock rim that defied any animal but a mountain goat — and again Jim was reminded that, if the mesa men were stealing K Cross beef, they would have to ford the river at Gray's Crossing.

He turned into the hotel dining room and sat down at a table near the window. Molly came in from the kitchen, the swinging door *swishing* shut behind her.

"Good morning, Jim." Molly wrinkled her nose at him. "You forgot to shave this morning."

Jim canted back his chair, gray eyes sweeping the girl's rounded figure. "You know why? I plumb forgot about you being here."

"How could you do that?" She shook her

28

head in mock despair. "I didn't think any-body forgot me."

"I don't rightly know how I could. Fact is, I didn't realize it was a good morning until you came in."

"Your blarney won't get you any extra flapjacks," she said tartly.

"My blarney! Say, who's Irish around here?"

"Not me. I'm an Eskimo, and I'm a hundred years old this morning. I suppose you want the usual?"

He nodded, only then noting that there was a soberness about her that was not like her. "The usual," he said.

Molly swung around, unable to restrain the neat wiggle of her hips that she had learned since she started working here. Jim grinned, thinking she didn't feel as old as she let on. Seeing her was a good deal like hearing a meadowlark's song when he woke up. It sweetened the day's beginning. The sour notes would come later.

Molly returned with a tray of flapjacks, ham, eggs, and coffee. She said: "The big moose is in town. Angela and Sam are with him." She set his food on the table and stepped back, somber eyes on him. "Will he ever get enough, Jim?"

"No, he never will," Jim answered. "Not

29

as long as he's alive."

"Then the Lord hasten the day when He'll send Klein where he belongs," Molly said, and walked away.

Jim ate slowly, thinking of what Molly had said and Angela's frank admission that she wanted to see her husband dead. Well, he'd die all right, probably from lead poisoning, and there would be no peace on Wild Horse River until he did.

The Kleins came into the dining room just as Jim was spooning sugar into his second cup of coffee, Holt Klein in front, Angela behind him, and Sam Pruett, the K Cross foreman, in the rear. Walking in front of his wife was typical of Klein, for he held an Indian attitude toward women, and Jim could understand how twelve years of this would be all that a wife could stand.

Klein's eyes fell on Jim. He scowled, muttered a grudging — "Howdy" — and moved on toward a table against the far wall. Pruett said in his usual courteous voice: " 'Morning, Jim." Angela nodded, smiling in a personal way as if she shared a secret with him, and went on toward the table Klein had selected. Pruett lingered a moment as if there was something he wanted to say, then he shrugged and followed Angela.

Molly came out of the kitchen, the usual flippancy entirely gone from her. She waited at their table, ignoring Klein's eyes that roved appreciatively from her red-brown hair down to her trim ankles and back. He said: "Ham-en-eggs."

Angela and Pruett gave their orders, and Molly stalked back to the kitchen, this time walking very stiffly. Jim rolled a cigarette, thinking of the gossip about Angela and Sam Pruett. After what happened last night, he could believe it.

Pruett was taller than Klein, but slighter of build, and, although Klein had imparted some of his insolence to his foreman, Pruett retained a courtesy of voice and manner that set him apart from his employer, at least to those he considered equals.

Klein sat in sullen silence, withdrawing himself from the other two in a manner that was typical of him. He was medium tall, but he gave an impression of bigness. His thick shoulders and hairy arms would have matched a blacksmith's for size. His eyes were dark brown, almost black, and they had a brutal way of staring a man down that forced obedience from most people.

For one short moment, Klein pinned his gaze on Jim's face, then he looked away. Jim had the feeling, as he had with Pruett when they had come in, that there was something Klein wanted to say. He wondered if either of them knew about Angela's visit to Pitchfork. He finished his coffee and rose, the hatred he had for Klein tying his nerves into knots.

Klein called: "Come here, Bruce!"

The man's voice always grated on Jim even when he was in a better mood than he was now. It held a disturbing gravelly quality that jarred his spine like metal scratching on metal, but more than that Klein had the habit of slapping a man with it as if he expected instant obedience. He had not been that way when he'd married Angela, but that was twelve years ago. This business of throwing his weight around had grown as his power and wealth had grown.

Jim remained motionless, cigarette stub pasted to his lower lip, a faint twist of smoke rising from it. He had never openly defied Klein, but such defiance must come and this was as good a time as any. Pruett looked a little scared; Angela's eyes were lowered, and, with a sharp stab of anger, Jim thought that she was saying to herself: *He's afraid.*

There was this one tight moment of silence, then Jim laughed. It was not a pleasant sound; it brought a greater worry into Pruett's handsome face and it forced

Angela to lift questioning eyes to Jim. Molly had come into the dining room from the kitchen with their plates of food. She stopped and stood there, tight-lipped, waiting.

"Holt," Jim said, "for a man who's made as big a splash as you have, you're a damned fool."

Klein's face turned red. For a moment he seemed to have trouble getting his breath, then he bawled: "What do you mean by that?"

"I've toted this star for a year," Jim answered, "and you know as well as I do that I've never jumped at your whistle like most folks do. What's more, only a fool would look for trouble when he's sitting at breakfast with his pretty wife."

Jim waited a moment, seeing the smug look of pleasure that flowed across Angela's face. Klein's mouth sagged open as if he had lost the power of speech. Then Jim turned and walked out, a grin coming to his lips. Angela might be thinking he had regretted what he had done the night before. Well, let her think it. She had thought she could use him, but, before this was over, it might work the other way.

For a time Jim lingered in front of the

hotel, eyes on the granite peaks of the Ramparts, and he found himself thinking of Linda Gale and her people who made a primitive living on the mesa, hemmed in by the Ramparts and Wild Horse River. He had received permission from Howdy Gale to ride through their country when he had run for sheriff, and he had shaken as many hands as he could, knowing all the time that they had no trust in him. Still, when the votes were counted, every man on the mesa had voted for him.

Jim threw his cold cigarette into the street and built another, standing there for no particular reason except that he knew he'd hear from Klein or Pruett. He could not get the mesa people out of his mind. He had never understood the reason for their withdrawal and their deep distrust for the flatlanders who lived across the river from them. Klein, he knew, was not responsible for it, because they had been that way as long as Jim could remember.

The minutes had piled up and still neither Klein nor Pruett made an appearance. A rider came into town from the west, gave Jim a cool nod, and turned into the livery stable. He was a stranger who called himself Smoke Malone, a weathered rail of a man who packed two guns, butts forward, and seemed to be completely indifferent to the trouble currents that flowed across the county.

From all the signs, Malone was a gunman — the kind, Jim judged, who hired out his .45 to the highest bidder. He had ridden into Harmony on a black gelding, and now, a month later, he was as mysterious as when he had first hit town. Apparently no one knew him, and he made no effort to get acquainted. He had taken a room in the hotel and spent most of his time in it when he wasn't riding, volunteering no information about himself or why he was here or where he had come from.

It struck Jim that it was strange Malone would be riding into town at this hour of the morning, for the black showed he had been ridden hard. Then Sam Pruett came out of the hotel, and Jim forgot Malone.

"Holt's been simmering ever since you stepped on his tail," Pruett said. "What was the idea?"

"What was his idea of yelling at me like I belonged to him?"

"Just his way. You know how he is. You'd better go in and smooth things up."

"Not by a damn' sight. You know something, Sam?"

"Yeah, I know something. You're

working yourself into a hell of a jam."

"I've been there ever since I got elected. I'm talking about something else. I'm gonna lick hell out of Klein. He's been overdue for a licking."

"You ain't man enough," Pruett said. "You've got enough trouble without going out looking for it."

Jim shook his head. "If I've made any mistake, it's been in not looking for it. I had that called to my attention last night."

He watched Pruett closely, wondering if the foreman had been responsible for Angela's visit the night before, but Pruett's expressionless face told Jim nothing.

"I don't savvy," Pruett said.

"Let it go," Jim said. "What did Angela say after I left?"

Pruett seemed puzzled. "You mean Missus Klein?"

Pruett was overplaying his hand, and now the suspicion deepened in Jim's mind that there was a connection here. "That's right. I mean Missus Klein."

"Oh, she didn't say much. Something about you being the only man in the county who'd talk to Holt that way."

"I reckon she was right about that," Jim said, and, wheeling, stalked down the street to his office.

He had intended to ride out to Gray's Crossing as soon as he had finished breakfast, but he had not counted on his run-in with Klein. There was no hurry about getting out to the Crossing. He'd wait, just to be sure whether Klein would push or drop it.

Jim sat down at his desk and thumbed through his Reward dodgers for the twentieth time, hoping he would recognize Malone's face. The fellow bothered him because he didn't fit into the pattern of trouble that Jim understood. Nobody on Wild Horse River had money to hire a gunhand except Klein, and Klein already had plenty of men on his payroll who could make a gun talk fast and fatally.

He shoved the stack of papers forward, shaking his head. No, Klein hadn't brought Malone here. He felt sure of that. On the other hand, he was equally sure Malone wasn't in the county for a vacation. Someone had hired him, but Jim was no closer to identifying that someone than he had been a month ago.

Leaning back in his swivel chair, Jim rolled a smoke, considering the gossip about Angela and Sam Pruett. Even if it wasn't true, Klein should be able to see what he was doing to Angela. He made it difficult, if not impossible, for her to have any women friends, and, if the blue dress she'd worn at breakfast was new, it was probably her first one in years.

He rose and paced the length of his office. Klein's and Angela's family trouble was none of his business, although Angela had tried hard enough to make it so, but Klein's threat about clearing Banjo Mesa *was* his business. If Jim could only be sure that the talk about K Cross losing beef was not true. . . .

"Bruce." It was Klein, standing in the doorway, his bulky body almost filling it. Jim wheeled to face him, gray eyes searching the man's brown, stubborn face and finding no enmity there. Just a mild curiosity.

"Well?"

"I've got some respect for you, Bruce. About like I'd respect an old mossy horn that hides out in the scrub oak at fly time."

"Now that's more than I expected. I don't hold the same respect for you."

Klein shrugged. "Every man to his own opinion. . . . But that ain't here or there. I've held back, thinking you'd turn up some rustlers, but you've done nothing, so I've made up my mind. You're resigning by the end of the month."

"The hell I will."

"You'll resign, all right. I've been on your tail all year about that Banjo Mesa bunch, and they're still there."

"Klein, I took all day yesterday riding along the creek, and I didn't turn up anything. I'm going up to Gray's Crossing this morning and talk to Dobe. If he hasn't run onto something, I'm gonna be sure of something I've been suspicioning."

"What's that?"

"That you ain't losing any beef."

Klein folded his thick arms across his chest, big head tipped forward. He was silent for a moment, dark eyes probing Jim's face in the arrogant way he had. Then he said: "I make out that you're getting around to calling me a liar."

"You can take it that way." Jim sat down on his desk, long legs stretched in front of him. "Holt, did it ever occur to you that I had a reason running for sheriff?"

"Hell, there ain't no secret about your reason. You couldn't make a go of your spread, so you wanted an easy job that'd keep you in beans and bacon. And I reckon you liked the feeling of being big that comes from toting the star."

"You're wrong, Holt. There's a little more to it than that. My folks were in the valley a long time before you were. So was

39

Tim Ryan. I rode by his place last night. His cabin's still standing there."

"I know that," Klein said, puzzled.

"I don't think you do. Not what it really means, because you never had a thought that wasn't about yourself and for yourself. You don't know about the blood and sweat that goes into a little outfit like Tim's and mine. Maybe you did once, but you've forgotten. . . ."

"I ain't forgot, but there's one difference. I went ahead. You didn't."

"I was a kid when we came here," Jim went on, ignoring the interruption, "but I remember how it was then. We had neighbors who were neighbors . . . the kind who came to weddings and helped with the chores when somebody was sick and gave a hand at the buryings. Folks like Tim and Lizzie Ryan."

"You're using a lot of words not to say anything," Klein jeered.

"I'm saying something, Holt. I found Tim lying in the willows along the creek. Remember?"

Klein's heavy-muscled face was stirred into a show of interest. "I remember. You trying to say I had a hand in that killing?"

"You had a hand in it, all right. Clear up to your elbow. If I'd been sheriff then, it

40

might have been different, but that's water under the bridge. You've taken a long time to run the little fry off the grass between the creek and the mountains, and you've never quite done the job. Molly still owns her quarter section, and I'm hanging onto my land. We're going back there someday, and we'll put cattle on the grass you claim is yours. What are you going to do about it?"

"I'll do plenty when that time comes." Klein fished a match out of his vest pocket and chewed on it. "So you're wearing the star to save money to buy cattle to buck me. That it?"

"That's it, and meanwhile I'm hoping to hell I can turn up something that'll give me a good reason to throw you into the jug till you rot or they hang you."

Klein laughed. "Just keep on hoping, mister. You never will." He cuffed back his sweat-stained Stetson. "I'll tell you what, Bruce. Like I said, I've got some respect for you. No sense in us bucking each other. I'll let you have a herd for a small down payment, and I'll tell Delaney to give you credit at the store. Might even get Waldron to make you a loan."

"What's the string?"

"No string, Bruce. Just your star, and you go back to ranching."

Jim shook his head. "No dice. The first time I missed paying my interest, I'd be broke. I'm kind o' sentimental, Holt. I'll go it alone, and I'll lick you. Maybe I can't do it by hanging you for the men you've murdered, so I'll wait."

"For what?" Klein asked contemptuously.

"For your cussedness to catch up with you, which is about to happen. Folks can forgive you for making money and being as big as all hell, but they can't forgive you for keeping 'em down on their knees."

No one, as far as Jim knew, had ever talked to Holt Klein like this. He had a faint hope that the K Cross owner would reach for his gun, but Klein had long ago learned that it was cheaper and safer to hire his fighting done. Not that he was afraid. It was a simple business proposition. The only life that mattered to him was his own.

Klein spit his match out, unruffled. "You're talking tough this morning, but it won't get you nothing. I always worked on the notion that it was cheaper to buy a man than kill him. You've had your chance and you've turned it down, so we're back where we started from. You clear Banjo Mesa of the bunch that's up there, or I will, and I'll have your star, to boot."

"And I'll have you in the jug if anything happens to the mesa bunch. Those people are the only free ones left on Wild Horse River. I reckon that's why you want 'em moved out."

Impatient now, Klein said: "Hogwash. I want 'em out because I'm losing beef and the mesa is an outlaw hang-out."

"You can't prove that, and neither can I." Jim shook his head. "They're staying until we can."

"So you sit on your rump and send a deputy up there who ain't dry behind the ears. Maybe you ain't neither. Or maybe you're in cahoots with the mesa outfit."

Jim rose. "I told Sam I was gonna lick hell out of you someday. Maybe this is the day."

Klein stepped out of the doorway. "You never saw the day you could lick me, but if you want to try. . . ." Klein stopped and swung around to see who was coming. In that same instant, Jim heard the hoof thunder of a running horse. He lunged through the door and stepped past Klein. It was the deputy, Dobe Jackson, riding like a crazy man.

Jim ran into the street as Dobe pulled his lathered horse to a stop, the dull red dust of the street whipping up around him. Dobe gripped the saddle horn, reeling a little, and it was then that Jim saw the dark patch of dried blood on his shirt.

"You're hit." Jim reached up. "Get the doc, Klein."

"Wait, Jim. I've got to talk. You light a shuck for Gray's Crossing. Last night somebody drove a bunch of K Cross cows down to the river and shot 'em. The calves are gone."

Sam Pruett was standing beside Klein now, and other men drifted up, attracted by Dobe's ride into town. Klein said loudly and with malice: "There's your proof, Sheriff. The mesa outfit knew they couldn't work over the K Cross brand, so they make mavericks out of the calves."

"That ain't all," Dobe whispered. "Old man Gray's dead. Got a slug . . . in . . . his . . . head."

Then the lights went out for Dobe Jackson, and he spilled from the saddle into Jim's arms. "Damn you, Klein!" Jim shouted. "I told you to get Doc Foster."

Jim carried Dobe into his office and laid him on the cot in the little side room where Dobe slept when he was in town, and he was thinking of the satisfaction in Klein's voice when he'd said: "There's your proof, Sheriff." A few cows and calves would not be too great a price for Klein to pay, if he could force Jim to arrest the mesa men, Howdy Gale and his brothers and the rest of them. Even the life of old man Gray would not be too much.

Jim waited there beside Dobe's still body, looking down at the boy's pale face. For a long time trouble had thrown a shadow across Wild Horse range. Now the shadow was gone and the trouble was here. And in the few bitter moments that it took Doc Foster to get there, Jim wondered what he could do. This morning he had used hard words on Holt Klein, but the showdown he sought had not come. Then he remembered Angela, and the thought occurred to him that Holt Klein's wife might be the one who could put a rope around Klein's neck.

Chapter Three

Pudgy little Doc Foster bustled in, black bag in hand. Others followed — Colonel Jarvis Steele, the lawyer, George Waldron, the banker, Pete Delaney, who owned the Mercantile, and a few more.

"Stay out there," the medico ordered brusquely. "Jim, give me a hand."

Klein, angry now, shouted: "Damn you, Bruce, there's a dozen men here who can help the sawbones, but you've got to do it while the rustlers that stole my calves are getting farther back onto the mesa all the time!"

Ignoring him, Jim helped the doctor strip the shirt and undershirt from the unconscious deputy. Foster examined the wound, and ran a hand around the boy's back. "Could be worse," he said, straightening. "A clean hole. Bullet went on through. Most of the damage is shock and loss of blood. A gritty kid, Jim. Made up his mind to get here to you and he did."

"I've got to talk to him, Doc."

Foster shook his head. "If you've got business somewhere else, get at it. Dobe's

46

gonna need plenty of rest. He won't be doing no talking for a while."

Nodding, Jim swung around. "You and Sam get your horses, Holt," he said, and pushed his way through the crowd into the street.

"Will the boy make it?" Colonel Steele called in his soft-toned voice.

Steele was in his sixties, but as straight-backed as most men half his age. He wore his white hair long; his mustache and goatee, as white as his hair, were kept carefully trimmed, and, judging from his clear blue eyes and unwrinkled skin, he had no worries of any kind.

Jim turned back, wondering why it was Steele who had asked. A dozen townsmen had jammed into the office, and all except Steele had seemed deeply concerned. But the lawyer was seldom concerned about anything. Jim had often wondered why the man tarried in Harmony. He had come more than a year ago when the only lawyer in San Marcos County had died, and he had stayed. Apparently he had money, he was well educated, and he had been all over the world, but there was something about this isolated range country that held him.

"I think Dobe will be all right," Jim said, and went on toward the Buckjack.

The other townsmen — Waldron and Delaney and the rest — had been in Harmony for years; they had seen Holt Klein's power and fortune grow, and with that growth they had felt the pressure of his overweening pride and increasing ambition. Now they were wondering where it would end and how it would affect them, but Steele, a newcomer, would not understand.

Jim found Smoke Malone playing solitaire in the Buckjack. As Jim came up to his table, he said in his flat-toned voice: "Howdy, Sheriff."

"Where were you last night?" Jim asked bluntly.

Malone laid his cards down and scooted his chair back. His eyes were pale and without expression; there was no reading them, yet the feeling was in Jim that the gunman was thoroughly dangerous. Now Malone fished tobacco and paper from his shirt pocket, staring coolly at Jim, then he lowered his gaze and rolled a smoke.

"Sheriff," Malone said, "I like most folks, but there's one kind of jasper I can't stand. That's a damned nosey lawman."

"I don't like 'em most of the time, either," Jim agreed, "but a man was murdered at Gray's Crossing last night, and you rode in from that direction early this morning."

48

"A man gets murdered, and you got yourself a hunch I done it." Malone shook his head. "You're making a bad mistake, friend, I ain't above killing a man, but when I do, it's in front of everybody."

"I still want to know where you were."

"None of your damned business," Malone said tonelessly. "I've got nothing against you, Sheriff, but don't crowd me. Take my word for it. I had nothing to do with the killing."

Jim felt a muscle jerking in his right cheek the way it did when anger gripped him, but he held it under a tight rein. He had no real evidence against Malone. The man was capable of murder, he had ridden in from the direction of Gray's Crossing, and he refused to account for his activities of the night before. It was enough to arouse suspicion, but not enough to make an arrest on.

"All right," Jim said evenly. "That's good enough for right now. I'm going out to the Crossing. Want to ride along?"

Malone rose. "Sure. Might even give you a hand if something comes up."

They left the saloon, Jim asking: "Your horse in the stable?"

"Yeah, but I'll get a livery animal. Mine's tuckered."

Neither Klein nor Pruett were in sight. A

sudden impulse struck Jim when they reached the hotel. "Go ahead and get your horse," he said. "I've got an errand in here."

Malone gave Jim a questioning glance as he turned into the hotel, then the gunman shrugged and went on to the livery stable.

The clerk was not at the desk and the lobby was empty. Jim glanced at the register. Klein had signed for Room 22. Probably Angela was in the room now. It might be difficult to explain his visit if Klein was with her, but it was a chance he had to take.

Jim climbed the stairs and turned along the hall. No one was in sight and he was glad of it, for he was ashamed of what he was doing. Duplicity did not come easily to him. He found Room 22 and knocked.

"Who is it?" Angela called.

"Jim."

She opened the door at once, and he saw that she was alone. She closed the door, saying softly: "So you did come."

"I'm here, all right."

"And you showed me this morning you aren't afraid of Holt." She stood close to him, her face upturned, the soft-lipped smile lingering in the corners of her mouth. "But it was just a gesture, Jim. Like shaking your fist at a mean bull."

"I've got to go. Dobe just rode in, shot all

to hell, and old man Gray's been murdered. I'm riding up there with Holt and Sam."

"You can't do that, Jim." She put her hands on his arms, frightened. "They'll kill you."

"I'm sheriff, Angela. I've got to go."

"No, Jim." She put her arms around him and clung to him, her face against his shirt. "We could have so much together, and you're throwing it away, because you're a fool, just a lovable fool."

He kissed her and she pressed him with a desperation that was close to panic. For that moment he was almost convinced that she meant what she said. He held her in his arms and felt the pressure of her breasts; he tasted the sweetness of her lips, and suddenly he was filled with hunger for her. Then he realized that was exactly what she wanted.

He pushed her away and reached for the doorknob, muttering: "I've got to go."

"Jim, don't you understand?" She caught his hand and pulled it back from the knob. "I couldn't sleep last night, wondering how soon you would come to me. I was afraid you'd wait too long. It isn't enough to love a man, Jim. A woman has to know she's being loved by him. Then this morning" — she laughed softly — "I knew that you were telling me you weren't afraid of Holt. If he was dead. . . ." She stopped as if shocked by what she had come close to saying.

Jim said: "K Cross would be yours."

"All right, Jim, let's be honest. K Cross would be mine, and I'd be free to marry a decent man, somebody who doesn't think that a woman is just a piece of flesh that he owns. And something else, Jim. You'd have peace on this range and people could live without being afraid. You wouldn't be finding men like Tim Ryan murdered. And old man Gray. Wouldn't it be worth . . . ?"

She lowered her head, still unable to put it into words, but no man, if he were a man, could remain indifferent to her, even when she was talking about murder as she was now.

He said: "I've got to go. . . ."

"No. Send Holt and Sam. Then you come back up here. I can't lose you now."

"I can't come here," he said a little roughly. "You ought to know that."

"Come out to K Cross then. Tomorrow. Or the next day. Holt isn't home in the day-time."

"All right. But I can't duck out on this job." Again he reached for the doorknob, then he remembered to ask the question he had meant to ask at first. "Where was Holt when you rode out to Pitchfork yesterday?"

"Playing poker in the Buckjack." She stepped back, her hands fisted at her sides. "I'm never as important to Holt as other things. He forgot all about me until he came in after midnight."

"Did Sam know where you were?"

"Sam!" Her eyes widened. "What are you trying to say, Jim?"

"Did he know?"

"Of course not. You think I tell my feelings to my husband's foreman?"

She had every appearance of telling the truth. He wondered if she had heard the gossip that linked her with Sam Pruett.

"I've got to go." He opened the door, saw that the hall was empty, and turned back to her. "I'll see you before long."

Her lips were trembling. She put a hand out toward him and dropped it, shaking her head. "Be careful, Jim. Will you do that much for me?"

"Sure, I'll be careful." And turning, he strode along the hall to the backstairs that led down to the alley.

He started running toward his house, realizing only then that he had broken out into a cold sweat. He had been a fool ever to think he could use Angela to put a rope around Holt Klein's neck. She would never come out in the open about it; she would use a man to achieve her ends, then she would break him and throw him away when she was done with him.

Mounting, Jim rode into the street, and, when he came into the business block, he saw Klein and Pruett waiting for him in front of the livery stable. Before he reached them, Klein shouted: "Where the hell have you been?"

"Getting my horse."

"You must have been making the saddle. You're about the poorest excuse for a sheriff I ever seen toting a star . . . so damned slow. . . ."

"All right. Holt," Jim said, dry-lipped. With his temper as thin as it was now, he was in no mood to take anything from anybody. "I told you a while ago that I aimed to give you a licking. Keep that tongue of yours from wagging, or I'll do it now."

"Let it go, Holt," Pruett said softly. "He's here."

Klein gave Jim a long look. He said then: "I'll let it go, for now." He motioned to Smoke Malone, who was standing in the archway of the stable. "This *hombre* says he's going along for the ride. Is that right?"

"That's right," Jim said. "Got your horse, Malone?"

"Yeah. But the big noise here says you don't need me."

"I'm needing a deputy," Jim said, "with Dobe laid up like he is. Get your horse."

Klein cuffed back his sweat-stained Stetson, his muscle-ridged face filled with the deep rage of a domineering man who finds himself unable to achieve his end.

"This is the damnedest thing I ever heard of," Klein said hotly. "What do you know about this gunslinger? You know enough to make him a deputy?"

"Maybe," Jim said.

Malone joined them, riding a livery-stable horse, and they turned westward, leaving town at a brisk pace. There were a number of men on the street, Waldron and Steele and some others, surprised and a little amused by the way Klein had been handled. In these few seconds, Klein had lost some of the prestige that was so important to him. He was left with the choice of following or staying in town, and he followed, his face ugly with the impotent fury that gripped him.

Jim did not look back, but he knew what he had done to Klein and he gained a grim satisfaction from it. Angela crept back into his thoughts. He remembered her saying that the only setback Klein had received since she had married him was his failure to control the election. That, Jim thought, was true, and now Klein did not know quite how to handle the situation.

The town dropped behind. Malone glanced sideways at Jim, asking in a low voice: "Not very smart to give Klein our backs, is it?"

"I figure he's stopped for the time being," Jim said.

"Maybe, but you didn't settle nothing. I never cottoned to looking down a bear's throat. You have to get so damned close to his teeth."

"The trick," Jim said, "is to pull your head back in time."

Malone was silent for a moment. Then he said: "Quite a notion you had, making me a deputy. I've tried my hand at a lot of things, but toting a star is something new."

"It ain't a bad idea if it'll show me which side you're on. We've all been wondering about that."

"Hell, I ain't on anybody's side, but there's one thing you can count on. I ain't on Klein's side."

They rode in silence then, Klein and Pruett keeping well behind. The day grew hotter as the sun crawled up into a brassy sky. The road paralleled the gorge, but at

56

this point it appeared to be only a slight break in the sage flat. A stranger, unless he rode to the rim and looked down at the twisting, plunging stream, would never guess that it formed an impassable barrier between the valley and Banjo Mesa.

They were climbing steadily, the piñons and cedars thicker and larger here in the higher altitude. Northward the valley dropped away, to spread for miles in endless monotony, until it gave way to the broken desert country with its arroyos and dry, windswept mesas. Beyond the desert, made hazy by distance and the shifting heat waves, were the San Juan Mountains. Later, an hour or more from the time they left Harmony, they came in sight of the K Cross buildings set at the base of the Ramparts to the north.

It was not yet noon when they reached Gray's Crossing. Here, for a quarter of a mile, Wild Horse River temporarily lost its character to flow past Gray's cabin in placid indifference to the falls and whirlpools that lay both above in the mountains and below in the gorge.

They reined up, Klein cursing in a bitter voice. It was easy enough to see what had happened — too easy, Jim thought. Twenty or more cows and calves had been driven

57

from the aspens above the cabin, the cows had been shot, and the calves pushed on across the river. It was not a new trick, and it was far safer than trying to alter the K Cross brand on the cows.

It was natural to assume that some of the Banjo Mesa bunch had done the job. By now, they would have slapped their own irons on the calves and pushed them far back into the broken country above the Red Wall. It would probably be impossible to find them, and even more difficult, if they were found, to establish Klein's ownership.

Hipping around in his saddle, Jim ordered curtly: "Stay on this side until I find Gray's body."

The cabin stood above the ford on a bench overlooking the river, a clump of aspens directly behind it. Jim rode toward it, paying no attention to Klein and Pruett, who had dismounted and were looking at the slaughtered cows. Reining up, Jim dismounted and circled the cabin on foot, finding no tracks or empty shells or anything that might point to the identity of the killer.

Jim came around to the front door and found it ajar. He waited until Malone rode up and dismounted, thinking about the door. Then he decided that it meant nothing, for he remembered that Dobe Jackson had found the body. The boy had been too excited to think about shutting the door, and that brought to Jim's mind the question of how and when Dobe had been shot.

"Where do you reckon your deputy was when this happened?" Malone asked.

"I wish to hell I knew," Jim said, and went into the cabin.

The interior was scrupulously clean, the way old man Gray had always kept it. Jim had stopped to visit whenever he happened to be close to the Crossing, and usually he had eaten with the lonely old man, who had welcomed any visitor with an eagerness that was pathetic.

Jim paused just inside the door until his eyes became accustomed to the gloom, then he saw the body on the bunk, and crossed the room to it. The old man always slept in his clothes, with just his hat and boots removed. He was that way now, a single blanket pulled over him. He lay on his side, a bullet hole above his right eye.

Malone moved up to stand beside Jim. "How do you read it, Sheriff?" he asked.

"I don't. I didn't get much out of Dobe before he fainted. I could come a lot closer to figuring this out if I knew what he knew."

"Damned funny deputy," Malone grunted. "Why didn't he stop it?"

"Maybe he wasn't here."

"Then why wasn't he?"

"Dunno. I told you I didn't get much out of him."

"Looks plain enough, anyhow," Malone said thoughtfully. "I'm guessing his visitor was someone he knew. Gray was in bed. Might have been sick. Somebody comes in to pay his toll. The old boy turns over to face the door and his visitor lets him have it."

Jim nodded. "Yeah. Plain enough except for who done it and why."

"You got any notions?"

"No, but the last time I was up here the old man was uneasy. Howdy Gale and his neighbors had heard Klein's talk about running 'em off Banjo Mesa, and Howdy was figuring they'd better hit K Cross before Klein hit them. What's more, several K Cross riders had been hanging around here, but Gray didn't know what they were up to."

"So he was expecting trouble."

"He saw it coming all right, and he knew he was sitting in the middle of it, but he was too stubborn to get out. He said he was gonna lock his door and sleep with his six-gun handy."

"There's no gun in sight." Malone felt around the body and stepped back, shaking his head. "Maybe the killer took it with him. Well, we've got to get him to town."

"He's got a team and buckboard in the shed," Jim said. "We'll hook up and fetch it around here."

They went out of the cabin together, Jim noticing that Klein and Pruett were still looking at the dead cows. A few minutes later, Jim drove the buckboard to the front door, Malone in the seat beside him.

"I'll tote him out," Malone said, and, stepping down, walked around the back of the rig and went into the cabin. A moment later he called: "Come here, Sheriff!"

Jim hesitated. Klein and Pruett were riding toward the cabin. Klein's face was thunder-dark. Jim could guess what Klein was going to demand, and the only answer he could make would be no. Anything could happen after that.

Malone called again, his voice sharp with impatience. "Sheriff, you'd better get in here."

Jim went in, not liking it, for Klein and Pruett would soon reach the cabin. He asked: "Find the gun?"

"No, but I found something else interesting as hell. Started to pick him up and,

61

when I got his head off the pillow, I found this." Malone handed a small dark object to Jim. "Whoever done the job left his signature."

"Take him out to the buckboard. I'll fetch a quilt to cover him."

Jim moved to the window as Malone carried the body outside. He examined the thing Malone had given him, turning it over in his hand and rubbing his fingertips across it. Smooth and coal-black except on the edges where it had been chipped thin. He held it up to the light. Along the edges it was translucent, like a piece of colored glass.

He slipped it into his pocket and, taking a quilt off the bunk, went outside, puzzling over it. He was not quite sure whether it was glass or rock. Perhaps Gray had it all the time, some sort of keepsake, but, whatever it had come from, Jim could see no sense in Malone's statement that it was the killer's signature.

When he reached the buckboard, he spread the quilt over the body and tucked it in, saying in a low tone: "Don't tell Klein about what you found." He stepped away from the rig and faced Klein, who had reined up twenty feet downslope from him.

"Turn up anything?" Klein asked.

"Not much. Gray was shot through the

head. We're taking the body into town."

"Malone can do that," Klein said thickly. "You're running my calves down."

Shrugging, Jim mounted and put his roan across the river and up the steep road that led to the top of the mesa. There had been no rain for several weeks, and the dust was three inches thick. Jim could tell nothing from the tracks except that the calves had been taken this way.

He turned back, certain that there was no use to follow them. The thieves, no matter who they were, would not stay on the road, and following them through the scrub oak jungle that covered much of the mesa would be slow at best. Now, making a quick decision, it seemed to Jim that these next few hours could be used to better advantage for another purpose. Then he reached the river and crossed it again, and saw that the trouble he'd asked for earlier in the day was here.

"Well, Bruce," Klein said ominously, "you've got plenty of proof now I wasn't lying to you. What are you going to do about my calves?"

"Nothing right now. There's some things about this deal that don't figure out right, no matter how many times I add 'em up."

"I figured you'd say something like that,"

Klein said in the same ominous tone. "You've fiddled and faddled, and every minute of your fiddling and faddling has given the rustlers a chance to get farther away. I say you're going after 'em."

Jim shook his head. "I'll play this my way, Holt. I'm going to town and talk to Dobe. Then I'm coming back."

"The hell you will. You're going now."

Jim shook his head again. "I was born stubborn, Holt. I'll find out who took them calves, but not today. I've got several notions about this. You've been after my scalp for a long time. Maybe you had this job done, figuring you'd get me to sashay around over the mesa and Howdy Gale would bust me out of my saddle."

Klein shot a quick questioning glance at Pruett. The foreman nodded. They were twenty feet apart, right hands close to gun butts. Klein was fast with his gun, and Pruett was supposed to be the deadliest gunslinger on Wild Horse River. Jim might be able to take him, but if he did, Klein would have time to spare. Even with the best of luck, Jim knew he wasn't fast enough to get both of them.

"That tops it all," Klein breathed, "saying I stole my own calves and butchered my cows. Maybe you think I killed Gray."

"Maybe you did. Somebody plugged him because he'd seen too much." Jim motioned toward Pruett. "Don't do what you're thinking, Sam. I'm pretty fair with an iron, fair enough to shake out one slug before you drill me, and it'll be your boss who gets that slug."

Klein bit his lower lip, glancing again at Pruett. There was no doubt he understood Jim's intentions, but he had gone too far now to back down. He said: "Change your mind, Bruce. Play this right and you can keep your soft job for a long time."

"I aim to play this right, Holt, and, before I'm done, I'll see you swinging on the end of a rope."

It would have come then if Malone had not called: "Don't try it, Klein! I've taken quite a shine to the sheriff."

Klein hipped around in his saddle and saw that Malone had pulled his gun. He turned back to Jim. "All right, Bruce. You've called me a liar today . . . you've said I stole my own calves and butchered my cows, and that maybe I killed Gray. I don't take that kind of talk from nobody. You're done on this range. Come on, Sam."

They wheeled their horses and headed for Harmony in a wild run, dust boiling up behind them. Jim rode up to the cabin.

"Thanks, Malone," he said. "I didn't figure on you buying into my trouble."

Malone grinned. "I always buy into trouble when it's as inviting as this is. I didn't think you were fast enough to smoke both of 'em down."

"I wasn't. Maybe I can return the favor someday." He fished the black object out of his pocket and held it up. "What is this? Might be glass or rock, but I can't tell which."

"Both. It's obsidian. Volcanic glass. Indians used to make arrowheads out of it. They'd swap it around and it'd wind up a thousand miles from where it started from. That piece might have come from the Yellowstone. Or eastern Oregon. Lot of it there."

"What did you mean about this being a killer's signature?"

"A man who hires out to do a job of killing might have to prove it was him who done the job, or he wouldn't get paid. Like Tom Horn, who'd put a rock under a man's head."

Jim stared at the obsidian, running a finger over the smooth, glass-like surface and thinking of what Malone had said. He dropped it back into his pocket and stepped down from the saddle, still unable to fit this into the pattern of trouble that had long been just below the surface here on Wild Horse range. He had mentally blamed everything on Holt Klein, but hiring a killer who had to mark his job didn't seem like Klein.

"I'll tie my horse on behind and drive this rig in," Jim said. "Go on if you're in a hurry."

"Hell, I ain't in no hurry," Malone scratched a cheek, pale eyes on Jim. "And I ain't telling you where I was last night or what I did. You still figger I had anything to do with this?"

"I ain't figuring anything just now," Jim said morosely as he tied his roan behind the buckboard. "I don't savvy it. I just don't savvy."

He climbed into the seat and spoke to the team. Malone looked at him questioningly, and, when he saw that Jim had said all he was going to, he reined in beside him. Jim stared ahead, the lines slack in his hands, remembering now that Colonel Steele had a rock collection and that Steele had been all over the country.

"This obsidian don't come from around here?" Jim asked.

Malone shook his head. "I don't think so. Never heard of it being found in this country."

There was silence again.

"You've got some notion running through your noggin," Malone said. "What is it?"

"I was thinking that this don't look like Klein's work."

"Funny thing," Malone said. "I was thinking the same."

Chapter Four

It was late afternoon when Jim and Malone reached Harmony. Malone turned into the livery stable; Jim went on down the street to Doc Foster's office and left Bill Gray's body in the medico's back room.

"How's Dobe?" Jim asked.

"Better'n he's got any right to be. He's been asking for you. Must have something on his mind."

"Is he alone?"

"No. Molly Ryan's with him."

"Then he'll be all right till I eat."

Foster grinned. "Sure, any man would be all right if he had Molly sitting with him."

Jim turned to leave, and then, quite casually as if it had almost slipped his mind, he said: "Doc, I'd like to get a few of the boys together."

"Something up?"

"Something's been up for a long time. What happened last night just brings it to a focus."

"It might not be smart, Jim. Depends on who you want rounded up."

"Pete Delaney and George Waldron. Tell

'em to be in Steele's office at five."

For a moment the medico stared intently at Jim's face. Then he asked: "Why?"

"Klein says I'm finished on this range and he's gonna have my star. I want to know where I stand."

"Hell, there ain't no question about that," Foster said quickly. "Klein ain't got a friend in Harmony."

"I want to find out if I have," Jim said, and wheeled out of the doctor's office.

Jim left Gray's rig and team at the stable and took care of his roan. He walked back uptown, ate a hasty meal at the Chinaman's, and then went directly to his office.

Molly rose from her chair at the side of the cot, motioning to Dobe's still body. "He's asleep right now, but he saw Klein leave town a while ago with Pruett and Angela, and he worried himself into a lather. He thought you and Klein had had trouble."

"We would have if Malone hadn't bought into the fracas. Klein allowed that two against two wasn't a good bet."

"No, he wouldn't," Molly said gravely. "He never made an even bet in his life." She smiled then. "Quite an occasion today. After you left town, Angela spent the morning in the Mercantile. When Klein

70

finds out how much he owes Delaney, he'll have indigestion for a week."

Jim stared down at Dobe's pale face, wondering guiltily if Molly knew he had been in Angela's room that morning. "Angela's had a hard time," he said. "I don't blame her for going on a buying spree."

Molly snorted. "All of you men are alike. Angela could make a fool out of any of you."

"Don't you feel sorry for her?"

"No. Not any sorrier than I do for Pruett or anybody else who has to live around Klein." She shook her head. "But his men seem to like him. I can't savvy that."

"He's a good cowman," Jim said, "and he pays good wages."

He was standing close to Molly. Now, looking directly at her, he thought she had the brightest blue eyes he had ever seen. Her lips were full at their centers and red, and there was a sweet set about them that was as natural as her gay laugh.

He thought with a sudden rush of regret that his life had been a barren one. There had been little time or place for a woman in it. He thought of kissing Angela and the quick wild hunger he'd had for her, and he found no pride in it. Molly was right. Angela would make a fool out of any man.

He looked down at Dobe again. "Did he

say anything about how he got shot or where he was when it happened?"

"No." She put her hand to her throat. "He's been a little feverish. Talks about . . . about Linda Gale."

There was no mistaking the misery that was in her eyes. It was the first time Jim had seen behind the gay, bantering mask she had worn since she had come to work in the hotel — and then he understood.

"You're in love with Dobe, ain't you?" he asked.

She stepped back, her gaze touching Jim's face and dropping. "Yes, I'm in love with him. But don't tell him. Don't ever tell him. He comes into the dining room and joshes me and once in a while he takes me to a dance, but I'm just another girl to him."

"He's young, Molly. Too young to think about getting married and settling down. Give him a little time."

There was no sound for a moment except Dobe's breathing, heavy and labored. Then Molly asked: "I've never seen Linda Gale. What's she like, Jim?"

Molly was jealous of the mesa girl. That struck Jim as being strange, for there couldn't be anything between Linda and Dobe. Or could there? The possibility raised a feeling of resentment in him, although he knew at once there was no reason for it. He had never had the opportunity to tell Linda how he felt, and Dobe didn't know.

"Kind of hard to say," Jim said. "I guess there's nobody else quite like her. You know how the mesa people are, wild as a bunch of Indians, and the Gales are the wildest of the lot."

"Is she pretty?"

"She would be if she was dressed up. Howdy Gale is Linda's brother, and you know what he is. Their folks are dead. Linda's the only girl in the family, and she dresses and acts like a man. I reckon she can do about anything a man can."

Suddenly Molly wheeled toward the door, calling back: "I've got to go to work. I'll send Missus Lane over."

He watched until she was out of sight, wondering about this discovery he'd made. It was exactly as he'd told Molly. Dobe was too young to think about love. A good kid who would someday make a first-class deputy, but he was far from that now. He'd made a mess of things at Gray's Crossing, and Jim admitted to himself that he was both surprised and disappointed. It was the first real test the boy had had, and he'd failed.

Jim sat down beside the cot and rolled a smoke. Presently Dobe stirred and turned over, his eyes open. His breathing was still labored, but Jim saw that the boy recognized him.

"Feel like talking?" Jim asked.

"Yeah, sure," Dobe whispered. "I'm no good, Jim. I'm resigning before you fire me. Gray would be alive if I'd stayed at the Crossing like you said to."

"Why didn't you?"

"Linda . . . she came down from the mesa. She . . . wanted me to go riding with her. I heard the shooting. Came back. Gray was dead. Cows were slaughtered. Somebody in the aspens got me. If I'd stayed. . . ."

"It's all right," Jim cut in. "You ain't resigning, and I ain't gonna fire you. I should have stayed there myself, but I didn't think anything like this would happen. Right now your job is getting well."

Dobe's eyes were shut again, and Jim doubted that he had heard. He stepped into his office, forced to recognize something he had not wanted to consider. The Gales, and that must include Linda, had been involved in the theft of the calves, and that led to another thought that was worse. Probably one of them had killed old man Gray and wounded Dobe.

It was after five when Mrs. Lane came. Jim said — "I think he's asleep." — and stepped out into the sunlight.

Colonel Steele stood in the doorway of his office, motioning with his hand. When Jim came up, he said with more sharpness than was usually in his voice: "We're here and waiting for you, Sheriff."

Irritation stirred in Jim as he stepped into the lawyer's office, nodding at Waldron and Delaney. Doc Porter sat in the rear of the room by himself, pulling on a blackened briar, his chair canted back against the wall.

"Maybe I should have called a town meeting," Jim said, "but I figured you boys were the ones who count. You've all got a stake here. More'n I have."

There was a moment of silence. Colonel Steele sat down at his desk, a long cigar tucked between his lips. Usually he was a talkative man, but now he was silent. Waldron, the banker, was small and sharp-eyed, and given to wearing expensive clothes that were out of place in a cow town like Harmony.

Delaney and Waldron were close friends, although they were as unlike as two men could be. The storekeeper was fat and bald with a repulsive face that harbored a wide blob of a nose and a drooping lower lip. He sat hunched forward, watery eyes on Jim, waiting. Only Doc Foster seemed unconcerned, knees crossed, the corners of his mouth holding a small smile.

"I don't know about having a stake," Steele said, leaning back in his swivel chair. "I came here because I wanted to retire and I liked the looks of this country." He picked up an agate paperweight and tapped it against his left palm. "Now a man's been murdered, a deputy shot, cows slaughtered, and calves stolen. I'm free to move out of here tomorrow, and I will if the law is not enforced."

"I'm just one man," Jim said. "My deputy is flat on his back and he'll be there for a while. Now let's get this straight. Holt Klein has run this country for a long time. He says he'll have my star, but I ain't one to resign when the job I set out to do ain't been done."

"I've got work to do," Waldron said sharply. "Why did you get us over here?"

"Yeah, that's what I want to know." Delaney's big body slid forward on his chair. "Just got in some boxes from Grand Junction that I've got to unpack."

Jim looked from one to the other, feeling their hostility and guessing what had happened. If there was a fight, these men had no stomach for a finish battle with K Cross. Certain that Klein would win, they refused to back a loser.

"So-oo," Jim breathed. "I get a smell that ain't good. As far as you're concerned, I can resign." He cuffed back his Stetson. "All right, you can go to hell, the whole bunch of you. You've been on your knees so long you ain't comfortable standing up like a man. All but Doc."

"A sawbones is different from anybody else," Doc Foster said. "I can afford to be independent. These boys figure they can't, Jim. I thought there was a backbone or two on Wild Horse River, but I was wrong. Just jelly that the Lord poured down their spines."

Angry, Steele leaned forward, his unlighted cigar held at a cocky angle. "I resent that, sir. I see no reason why I should get embroiled in a mess that is the sheriff's responsibility."

"I do," Foster snapped. "This mess is everybody's responsibility. I've known Jim most of his life. I was here before any of the rest of you. I remember the Bruces coming across the desert in a covered wagon and driving in a few head of cattle. Jim was just a button then. I remember the Ryans coming, with Molly a baby in her mother's arms. It was a hot day, and she didn't have nothing on but a didie."

"What the hell . . . ," Delaney began.

"Shut up, Pete," Foster said. "I told you I knew Jim better'n the rest of you. I know why he ran for sheriff in the first place. Want me to tell you?"

"I'll tell 'em," Jim said. "I was finished on my spread. Owed Waldron some money that he decided he needed, so I sold off everything I had and paid him off. Now I'm saving all I can and someday I'm gonna start over."

The medico shook his head. "There's more to it than that, Jim, and I'm aiming to make it damned clear right now. He's different from any of you. Take Delaney here. He dances to Klein's tune because Klein buys his supplies from him. If he stopped dancing, Klein would ship his supplies in himself and Delaney would lose his biggest customer. That right, Pete?"

"I don't aim to buck him," Delaney muttered.

"I can see that," Foster said witheringly. "Same with Waldron. If Klein pulls his money out of the bank, Waldron loses his biggest depositor. As for you, Colonel, I suppose that, if you didn't get Klein's legal business, and what the bank and Delaney throw your way, you'd starve."

Steele took the cigar out of his mouth. "I resent that, too, sir. I am not dependent upon the penny-ante business that is to be found in Harmony, and I have never at any time lost my pride to the extent of knuckling down to Holt Klein."

Foster spread his hands. "All right, Colonel. What I'm saying is this. All of you hated like hell to hear that Dobe Jackson had been shot. You hated it worse when you heard Gray had been murdered. Why? Because you said to yourself that, if real trouble starts, you'll lose your money, your business, and maybe your life. You hate Klein and you hate yourself, because you haven't got the guts it takes to make an honest stand and back a man who has got guts."

The doctor rose and knocked his pipe against his palm. "Instead of helping Jim whittle Klein down, you'll shove him out on a limb. Damn me, if I've ever seen a more contemptible, belly-crawling bunch of whelps than you."

Waldron jumped up, thoroughly angry. "I don't have to listen to you, Doc. A man has a right to look to his own interests. Bruce can look to his."

"You aren't going anywhere!" the medico

shouted. "I set out to tell you why Jim took the sheriff's star, and I'm going to do it. You've got interests, all right, but what are they? Dollars! That's what they are, and the closer you stick to Klein, the more dollars you'll make."

Delaney was on his feet beside Waldron, his flabby face scarlet. "Sure, our interests are money. I suppose Bruce is toting the star for fun?"

"Not exactly, but we all know he could have made a deal with Klein, like most of the boys have. But Jim ain't made that way. There's always been a few men who've had the guts it takes to fight greed and injustice, and that's the way it is with him. If it hadn't been for men like Jim Bruce, we'd still be living under kings and such."

"I'm surprised, Doc," Steele said, eyes faintly mocking. "I never suspected you were an orator. You should run for office."

"I'll bet my bottom dollar," Foster hurried on, ignoring the lawyer, "that every one of you voted for Jim. Why? Because you hoped to hell he'd bust Klein. You knew he'd try, but, when it comes to a showdown, you run like rats for your holes." The doctor rose and jammed his pipe into his pocket. "Come on, Jim. The air's plumb foul in here."

"Wait, Doc." Jim moved to Steele's desk. "There's some things I don't savvy about Gray's killing and them cows that was slaughtered. I figured I might get some help from you boys, but it don't look like I'm going to."

Waldron had dropped back into his chair, eyes on the floor. Delaney remained on his feet, sullen anger still working in him. Steele had regained his usual placidity, apparently unconcerned and superior to everything that had been said.

"Let's drift," Foster said irritably. "You won't get no help from a band of sheep when you talk about tackling a curly wolf."

"Not till I find out one thing." Jim tossed the piece of obsidian to Steele's desk. "What is that, Colonel?"

The lawyer picked it up, suddenly wary. "Obsidian. Where did you get it?"

"Where did it come from?"

"How would I know?"

"You've bragged some about your rock collection. I was thinking that, if it was as good as you let on, you'd have some obsidian."

"Certainly I have some. It comes from the high desert in central Oregon. I'll show it to you." Steele rose and walked into his back room. He was back an instant later, visibly shaken. "What is the significance of that piece you have?"

"I want to see yours."

Steele stood motionless, his back ramrod straight. His cheeks, ordinarily a healthy pink, had turned gray, as if his age had caught up with him during these few minutes. It was the first time Jim had ever seen the lawyer at a loss for words, the first time he had seen the cool air of superiority gone from the man.

"I can't show it to you," Steele said hoarsely. "I had several like the one you have." He swallowed, a hand coming up to rub across his hair. "They're gone, Sheriff. I . . . I seldom look at the cabinet where they were. They might have been gone for several days."

"Who knew about them?"

Steele glanced at Waldron and Delaney, and threw up his hands. "I don't know. I mean, I've showed my collection to a lot of people."

"As far as you know, you had the only obsidian in the country?"

"Yes." Steele swallowed. "I asked you what the significance of that piece . . . ?"

"One more question. Could this piece have come from your collection?"

"Sure, but one piece of black obsidian looks much like another. I couldn't be positive."

"This was under Gray's head." Jim picked up the piece from Steele's desk and dropped it into his pocket. "Malone says it's probably the killer's signature, so the man who hired him to do the job would know he was paying the right party."

Steele was angry then, bitterly and furiously angry. He took a step toward Jim, fists clenched. "Are you insinuating, sir, that I killed Gray or had him killed?"

"No, I ain't insinuating anything. I just don't savvy."

"I have no explanation to give you," Steele said stiffly.

"When you think of one, I want to hear it." Jim jerked his head at the door. "Come on, Doc."

They went out together, leaving the three men behind them sullenly silent. For a moment they stood in the sharp sunlight, neither speaking. Then the doctor took a long breath and shook his head.

"Well sir, you never know," Foster said in a low, bitter voice. "I thought you aimed to get hold of Klein and Pruett and cram something down their throats, and I figured that wouldn't be smart, things being what they are. Then you named these fellers, and I thought you'd find out the town was backing you . . . but that was the biggest mistake I ever made."

"It ain't such a surprise, at that," Jim said. "I always had a hunch Klein figured he'd run me out of the valley by having the bank collect them notes of mine."

Foster gave him a penetrating look. "You're too danged stubborn to quit, ain't you?"

"It ain't just a proposition of being stubborn. I can't quit."

"I reckon you can't," Foster said moodily. "But now you know one thing. You won't just be fighting Holt Klein. You're fighting everybody else in the county, because they're afraid to make a show against Klein. He'll let time work on you, and after a while you'll be so sick of carrying the load and having every man's hand against you that you'll quit."

Jim gave him a tight grin. "Not every man's hand, Doc."

Jim turned toward the livery stable and rented a pack animal. A few minutes later he rode out of town on his roan, leading the pack horse. He headed upriver toward Gray's Crossing, and he found himself wondering about Smoke Malone and his notion that the piece of obsidian was the killer's signature. It was quite possible that the gunman had wanted to turn his suspicion to Jarvis Steele.

Chapter Five

It was dusk when Jim reached Gray's Crossing. He circled the cabin, stopping often to listen, but there was no sound to indicate human presence. He rode on toward the aspens, and, by the time he reached them, it was fully dark, the blackness relieved only by a scattering of stars overhead and a thin moon showing in the east.

There was no definite plan in Jim's mind, but some things were clear. Waldron's and Delaney's hostility could be explained only by their fear of Klein's enmity, or that they were actually working hand and glove with him. Steele had been a puzzle from the day he had first come to Harmony, and he had said nothing this afternoon that had made his position clear. Only Foster had taken a stand, but Jim had known what to expect from him.

To Jim Bruce the oath to enforce the law was a sacred obligation. Now it was more than that. Old man Gray had been murdered, and only good luck had kept Dobe Jackson alive. It was a personal thing, for Jim had liked Gray and he thought of Dobe much as he would have thought of a younger brother.

Jim watered his horses and put hobbles on them. His mind had worked on the puzzle of Gray's murder from the time he had left town, but no amount of thinking had given him a sound explanation for it.

Klein was the natural suspect, although it didn't quite add up. It was easy enough to blame Klein for everything that was wrong, and Jim, as almost everyone else in the county had done for years, had fallen into the habit of laying every killing and theft that occurred on the K Cross man. But Gray had been an innocent bystander, a gnat buzzing in Klein's ear if he did aim to take over the Banjo Mesa range, and the conviction grew in Jim's mind that Klein was far too smart to kill a man for no better reason than the saving he would make by not having to pay Gray the few dollars it would take to shove his cattle across the river at this point.

Jim built a fire, forced to accept the possibility that someone else was at work here, perhaps even several people who had done nothing in the past to focus suspicion upon them. If that were true, there was nothing to do but wait.

He moved back into the shadows,

thinking that this was one night when he would go hungry. A man hunkering over a campfire made too good a target. He rolled and smoked a cigarette, listening for the sound of a moving horse. The fire was bait, and, unless he was completely off the track in his thinking, the bait would lure someone to him before dawn, perhaps Linda Gale. He viewed that possibility with mixed feelings; he hated to think that she had persuaded Dobe to disobey orders and go with her.

If, as Klein had said so many times, the mesa people were harboring outlaws or branching out into the rustling business, Gray would have been a witness. Still, no matter how much sense it made, Jim could not believe any of the mesa men had killed him. They had courage and their own strange sense of honor, and it was not like Howdy Gale or any of the others to kill a man the way old man Gray had been murdered.

Linda Gale was there before he knew anyone was around, her soft — "Howdy, Sheriff." — breaking into his thoughts and sending him rolling more deeply into the shadows as his right hand dug for his gun. She laughed as unabashedly as a child who has just put over a sharp trick. "Take a deep breath and straighten up. I'd have shot you ten minutes ago, if I'd wanted to."

He located her tall dark-garbed figure then, to his left deep among the close-growing aspens. He got to his feet. "Come on in. I just took that deep breath."

She laughed again, moving silently through the trees until she stood beside him. "You built that fire to fetch someone, didn't you?" she asked.

"That's right. I figured you might show up. Now I want to know who killed Gray and drilled Dobe last night."

"I had nothing to do with it," she said indignantly, "and I don't know anything about it. What makes you think I did?"

"You get around. I thought you might know something."

"I don't."

"That's good enough for me. Sit down. I'll build up the fire and make some coffee."

"No. Stay away from the fire. You never know who's around." She sat down, her back against an aspen trunk. "Trouble's coming, Jim."

He dropped to the ground beside her. "Trouble's here. Linda, you must have some notion about who killed Gray."

"No."

There was a moment of strained silence

between them. He stared at the pale oval of her face, picturing her bright black eyes, her black hair that she wore pulled back tightly from her head, the strong set of her features. She had a wild temper, she rode and shot like a man, and, if it came to a fight, she'd be just as good as a man.

Jim admired her more than any woman he had ever known, for there was a straightforward honesty and an inherent goodness in her that he had never found in another woman, not even in Molly Ryan. He remembered Angela Klein saying that, if he loved Linda, he'd be wasting it. Angela did not know Linda except by hearsay, but she was probably right. Jim could not remember a mesa woman ever marrying a flatlander. The fact that Jim was a lawman made his chances even smaller. The mesa people hated lawmen, even one they had voted for.

"Why are you here, Jim?" Linda asked suddenly.

"I've got a murderer to figure out, some rustlers to catch, and a bushwhacker to nab. Ain't that enough to fetch me up here?"

"Too much. I suppose Klein claims we did all of it, and he's going to run us out of the country."

"He sure figures you got his calves."

"And you're going to help him nail us for

90

it, aren't you?" she asked scornfully.

"No. I thought you knew me better than that."

"You didn't know me very well," she reminded him. "You thought I had a hand in Dobe's shooting and Gray's murder."

He was silent for a moment, wondering how well he did know her. The only chance he'd had to talk to her was when he'd been on the mesa before election. It had surprised the Gales and their neighbors that he'd had the temerity to come to the mesa seeking votes, and, because they placed a high value upon raw courage, they had permitted him to come and go as he had wanted. Howdy Gale had even appointed Linda his official guide the last three days Jim had been on the mesa. "Just to keep your head from getting blowed off," Howdy had said in a matter-of-fact voice.

"You do know something I need to know," Jim said finally. "Dobe got hit pretty hard and he didn't feel much like talking, but I got one thing out of him. He said you asked him to go riding, and he did. That's why he wasn't where I told him to stay when it happened."

"It wasn't just that way," she said stiffly. "I was supposed to get him away from the Crossing, but I wouldn't have done it if I'd known somebody planned to kill Bill Gray."

"Let's have the yarn."

"I can't tell you anything else, Jim."

She was stubborn. He knew her well enough to be sure that there was nothing he could say that would change her mind until she was willing to have it changed. He asked: "Why are you here tonight?"

"Just riding. I saw your fire and got curious." She paused, and then said with deep bitterness: "You're on the right side of things, aren't you, Jim?"

"What do you mean by that?"

"You know what I mean. People who amount to anything in this country stand in good with Klein. We're different. We don't have any friends if we step off the mesa. We never bank with Waldron. We never buy anything from Delaney. All we want is to be let alone. Is that asking too much, Jim?"

"No." He rolled a smoke, knowing that it was natural for Linda to think that he stood with Klein. He fired the cigarette, keeping the flame cupped with his hands, then blew it out. "I said a while ago I thought you knew me better than that. I tell you I'm not siding Klein."

"Doesn't he always tell the county officials how to jump?"

"Not me, he don't."

"You've toted that tin star for a year," she said tartly, "and Klein's still not in jail."

"Oh, hell," he groaned. "He ain't done nothing in the last year I could jail him on."

"He's fixin' to," she said. "I'll tell you why I'm riding tonight. More than a month ago Klein gave me an order. Sell out or get out. He needed our range. Since then we've had men posted on our side of the river. Howdy thinks that K Cross will ride in some night and burn us out."

"Might do it." He put out his cigarette. "Linda, I've got my reason for wanting Klein whittled down the same as you have, but I've got to have help."

She laughed. "You think you'll get help from us, do you? Howdy will love to hear that. Why don't you get help from your own people . . . Waldron and Delaney and that bunch?"

"They're not my people." He told her what had happened since morning, and added: "Doc's right about why I wanted this job. I've done a lot of thinking about how Klein is holding the country back. If we had a dam here on the river, we could ditch water down to the valley. It's good land, Linda. A hundred families could make a living between here and San Marcos Creek."

She laughed again. "You're dreaming, Jim. That's Klein's winter range you're talking about."

"Sure, just dreaming. Anyhow, it's me or Klein now, and my gun ain't enough. I don't even have Dobe to side me."

"And you're blaming me for that?" she cried.

"He was riding with you."

"All right, he was riding with me, but don't count on us to pull you out of the bog hole you got yourself into."

"I aim to have a talk with Howdy. I need his help, and I've got to make him see that the only way we'll ever have peace on this range is to make the law mean something."

"Don't show your nose on Banjo Mesa," she said. "You'll just get it shot off if you do. Howdy thinks you're Klein's man, and he cusses the day he voted for you. You'd better saddle up and light out for Harmony. Then maybe you'd best just keep on riding."

"My folks are buried in Harmony," he said. "I guess I'll hang around so they can plant me there, too."

"But why, Jim? You're a man. You don't have to stay in a country like this and risk your hide fighting a devil who runs every-thing. If I was a man. . . ." She stopped.

"Oh, well, that's crazy dreaming, too. I get downright provoked at the Lord for making me a woman."

"You'll be glad He did someday. You'll get married and have kids. . . ."

"The hell I will. Who is there on the mesa I'd marry?"

"All the men in the world ain't on the mesa."

"And who is there in this country who would marry a mesa woman? Nobody but a mesa man, and you know that's the truth. So I'll go on being a he-woman. I'll patch my brothers' duds and cook their meals and, after while, they'll plant me under some piñon tree. Now ain't that a hell of a way to spend eternity?"

He laughed. "I won't let that happen, Linda. I'll marry you myself."

"Don't say that, Jim," she said sharply, the good humor gone from her voice. "I was joshing, but when you say a thing like that. . . ." She stopped. Jim heard it, horses splashing across the ford. He got up and would have moved into the clearing if Linda had not grabbed his leg. "Hold on, you idiot," she whispered. "That's K Cross and there's a dozen in the outfit."

"I told Klein I'd put him in jail if he raided the mesa."

"Then you'd better sweep your cell out, mister, because that's just what he's up to." She started running through the aspens.

He called: "Wait for me at the cabin!" He didn't think she would, but, when he had saddled and ridden to the clearing, he found that she was there.

"There's a brush pile on Coyote Rock," she said. "I've got to fire it. Before we're done, Klein will think he's run into a wasp's nest."

She reined down the slope toward the ford, Jim beside her, the star shine falling across her dark face. He saw, and it came as a shock that she was enjoying it. In this way she was like her brother; she'd go ten miles out of her way to get into a fight.

They crossed the stream, the water silent here and touched by the thin light so that it looked like flowing silver, then they were out of it, their horses laboring up the steep slope. They stopped at the crest of the mesa hill to blow their horses, and Linda said: "Sounds like they're heading for Chinook's place. They'll kill him if they catch him asleep."

"It'd take an Injun to catch that old boy asleep," Jim said. "Get your fire going."

He reined his horse up the narrow trail that led to Lost Horse Cañon. She called to him, but he went on, not hearing what she said. This was no time for talk. Holt Klein had at last made the mistake of taking the law into his own hands, a mistake that Jim could not let go. Klein had made his threats, and Jim had told him what he would do if the K Cross owner carried them out. The sparring had lasted for a year. Now the sparring was over. The hour of decision was here.

It was nearly level country, the brush-lined creek to Jim's right, and he rode fast and recklessly. Whatever doubts these clannish people had of him would be dispelled tonight. Then he thought: *If I live.*

Nobody on Wild Horse River knew anything about the old man who called himself Chinook, not even his real name, or where he came from, or why he had come. He was typical of the mesa people in wanting to be let alone. His cabin was at the mouth of Lost Horse Cañon, one of the passages by which a man could thread his way through the Ramparts.

It was possible that Chinook made his living by guiding fugitives across the state line into Utah. Klein had made the charge often enough, but it was the sweeping accusation that Klein made against all the Banjo Mesa people. There was no more proof against Chinook than there was against the Gales or the rest of them. Chinook lived alone, his wants were few, and he was capable of supplying them by his Winchester and fishing pole.

If Linda had guessed right, K Cross would move cautiously against Chinook, warily working toward the cabin to surprise the old man. Perhaps it had been that way with Bill Gray, but here there was a difference. Chinook was a night owl who slept most of the day and prowled by night. It was still early, so he was probably puttering around his place by lantern light.

Jim almost reached Chinook's cabin before he attracted the attention of the night riders. A shouted bellow for him to stop came from the brush along the creek. He pulled his gun and fired a wild shot, a shot intended both as a gesture of defiance and a warning to Chinook.

Guns winked from the other side of the creek, bullets snapped by overhead, but he was hidden by scrub oak, and none of them came close. Then he saw a lighted lantern directly ahead, and he yelled: "Hit for cover, Chinook!"

Jim came out of the close-growing scrub oak and reached the clearing just as Chinook bolted for the barn in his awkward, loose-limbed run. He jerked the door open and blew out his lantern, and again guns roared from the creek bottom. This time slugs slapped into the spruce logs of the barn wall, one of them coming close to Jim's head; then he was inside and stepping out of the saddle as the old man slammed the door shut.

"Who are you?" Chinook demanded.

"Jim Bruce."

"The sheriff!" Chinook ejaculated. "Now if that ain't hell."

"What's hell about it?"

"Ain't that Klein's bunch out there?"

"I didn't see none of 'em, but it's my guess that's who it is."

"Then what are you doing here? You've got skunk smell on you just like the rest of the flatlanders."

"Take another whiff," Jim snapped. "Your smeller ain't working tonight. Got a gun on you?"

"Just my hogleg."

Jim lifted his Winchester from the scabbard and wheeled to the door. The firing had stopped. He shoved the door open, eyes probing the darkness that blanketed the clearing, but he could not catch any hint of movement. Then he saw the brush fire on Coyote Rock gleaming like a great star that lay close to the horizon.

"Linda's got the fire going," Jim said. "She allowed it'd fetch help."

"Yeah, if it gets here in time," the old man grunted. "How many's in this outfit?"

"A dozen, maybe."

Chinook groaned. "We can't hold off that many."

"I ain't so sure. Leastwise, we can make 'em pay plenty before they root us out."

Jim crouched in the doorway, studying the darkness and listening. The corrals were to his right, the cabin to his left directly above the creek. Behind the barn, not more than fifty yards away, were the first steep ridges of the Ramparts, rising sharply above the mesa.

The minutes passed slowly, each one dragging out like an eternity. There was no firing now, no sound of movement, and Chinook said hopefully: "Maybe they got skeered off when you rode in like a bat out of hell."

"Don't count on it," Jim said.

Chinook was doing a little wishful thinking. Jim could not guess what was in the minds of their assailants, but they would know there was only one man who had come to Chinook's aid. And if Klein intended to murder Chinook and destroy his place as a warning to the rest of the mesa people, his men would not quit this easily.

"It'll take an hour or more for anybody to get here," Chinook worried. "By that time we'll be deader'n two ticks in a barrel of sheep dip."

"Got any sacks of grain?"

"Yeah. Some oats."

"Let's pile 'em up here in the door so we'll have something to shoot over. Chances are they're bellying up and pretty soon they'll give us a rush."

"All right," Chinook grunted. "Reckon we'll go down kicking, but I've been through some ruckuses like this. If they really aim to make me a goat, they'll do it, come hell or high water."

"Hot lead's a discouraging argument," Jim said. "Let's get at it."

They moved the filled sacks to the doorway, piling them three high so that Jim, kneeling behind with the barrel of his Winchester shoved between the top sacks, had protection against anything except a lucky slug that might find the slot through which he had thrust his rifle.

"What's holding you?" Jim yelled. "We've got help coming."

"What the hell," Chinook said in a sullen

101

voice. "Of all the chuckle-haired idiots, you take the cake. Why can't you let them sleeping dogs keep on sleeping?"

Jim made no answer. He waited, hammer back, watching for movement, but the clearing, faintly lighted by the thin moon and the stars, seemed entirely deserted. Then, perhaps an hour later, the silence was wiped out by a sudden burst of gunfire. The attacking party had lined out along the creekbank, the red wink of their fire making an irregular line beyond the stream.

There were eight or nine bunched down there, Jim guessed, and for a moment he puzzled over this maneuver. It seemed crazy. They would burn up their ammunition if they kept this up, and still do no harm to the men inside the barn, unless they made some lucky hits. Then he guessed what they were up to. The firing from the creek had been designed to cover an attack from the rear.

"This the only door?" Jim asked.

"Yeah. Just a window on the other side."

"Get over there. If you catch anybody moving in from the brush, let 'em have it."

Chinook pattered across the barn to the other wall. A moment later he started shooting. A man screamed, and Chinook let out a triumphant squall. He crowed: "My eyes are still good, Sheriff! I got me a coyote."

Jim had no time to talk. Two men had reached the corner of the barn, moving in from the side, and now they dived over the oat barricade. Jim's rifle was lodged between the sacks. He jumped back, clawing for his Colt. There was a flurry of arms and legs, the *thud* of blows, and the wild, frantic oaths of men who had worked themselves into a killing frenzy.

If there had been only one, Jim would probably have died, but it had been a mistake to send two. They were in each other's way, and in the darkness neither could be sure which was the enemy. Jim had no such problem. He broke free while the other two were still tangled. His gun cleared leather as he rolled across the stable floor; he pronged back the hammer and let go with a shot just as one of the men jumped on him.

It was impossible for Jim to miss. One instant the fellow was smothering him, a knife blade slashing downward that caught his sleeve and buried itself into the dirt and barn litter. Then the man relaxed and blood spurted across Jim's arm and shoulder.

The second man was emptying his gun in the frantic hope that at least one slug would connect. But the dead man was still on Jim, a shield that saved his life. He felt the body jerk with the impact of a slug. Then he had worked his right arm free of the limp weight upon him and, clutching the dead man with his left, fired.

There was a moment of silence while the echoes of the shots faded, the air heavy with the smell of burned gunpowder. Chinook began babbling like a crazy man, not knowing how Jim had fared. Outside, the shooting had stopped.

"I'm all right!" Jim shouted. "Shut up, Chinook. Get over here and watch the clearing. They may figure this is the time to rush us."

Chinook obeyed as Jim struck a match and held it to the face of the first man he had shot. The fellow was a stranger. He thumbed another match to life, cupping the flame with his hand as he brought it close to the face of the second man. It was Red Landers, a K Cross cowhand.

Jim's first thought was that Linda had been right when she'd said this was Klein's move to enforce his order. Then he saw that Landers was not dead. The man was barely breathing, his life pouring out of him from a chest wound.

"What'd you make a fool play like this for?" Jim asked.

"They was gonna give a thousand dollars to the man . . . who got . . . you . . . two."

"Who was gonna give it? Klein?"

Landers made no answer, and for a moment Jim thought he was dead. Then Jim heard the labored breathing, and he said: "You're cashing in, Red. Better talk. Might go easier on you."

"Yeah, easy in hell. Ain't . . . Klein. It's Pruett . . . and . . . that . . . purty. . . ." Then Red Landers's voice faded out; he gave a choking sigh, and died.

"They're moving out!" Chinook yelled. "Hear them horses?"

Jim said nothing. He hunkered beside Landers's body, thinking about what the dying man had told him and trying to fit it into the pattern of human greed and selfishness that had plagued the Wild Horse range from the day Klein had moved in upon his neighbors. It had been natural enough to lay this raid at Klein's door just as Linda had done, but Landers had said it was not Klein, and there had been no reason for a dying man to lie.

Now Jim was forced to revise his thinking. There had been no one else to blame, but Landers had named Pruett, so Jim came to the only conclusion he could. Pruett was selling Klein out, taking advantage of his threat and the suspicion the mesa people had of the K Cross owner, but Landers had not lived long enough to tell why or what sort of game the foreman was playing.

Jim was still there, thinking about it, when Chinook shouted: "Linda's bringing 'em in, now that we don't need any help!"

Chapter Six

There were fifteen or more in the bunch that thundered into the clearing, Linda riding in front like a man. When they reined up, it was Linda who demanded: "Anybody hurt?"

"Yeah, you bet!" Chinook yelled. "Three of 'em. They're hurt so bad they're dead."

"What about Jim Bruce?"

There was a fine edge of worry in her voice that made Chinook cackle. "Naw, he's all right. A fighting rooster, that boy."

Jim found Chinook's lantern and lighted it. He came toward Linda, the murky light moving in weird shadowy waves across the yard as he held the lantern high.

"We're all right," Jim said, and told them what had happened. As he talked, his eyes searched the circle of riders for Howdy Gale, but the man was not there. He finished with: "I thought I knew every cowhand on this range, but one of the boys in the barn is a stranger to me."

"You say the other one's Red Landers?" Linda asked.

"That's right. Showed up about the time Pruett signed on to rod K Cross."

"It's enough to prove it was Klein who ordered this raid," Linda said doggedly. "I don't know why Landers lied, but that's what he did."

"I don't think so," Jim said.

"There's another one back of the barn," Chinook broke in. "I nailed him just when them other two jumped the sheriff, but I sure don't know what he was up to."

Turning, Jim walked in long strides around the barn, Chinook beside him. Reaching the dead man, he angled the lantern so that the light fell directly across the fellow's face. There was a can of coal oil on the ground beside him.

"That's what he was up to, Chinook," Jim said. "He was gonna burn us out." He wheeled, calling: "This *hombre*'s a stranger, too!"

Jim walked back to Linda and the others, wondering why Howdy was not with them. He had been the recognized leader of the mesa people for years, and now in his absence they looked to Linda for orders. They were a nondescript lot, varying in age from old men like Chinook, honed down by harsh living to hide and bone, to boys who were younger than Linda.

Now, his gaze sweeping the circle again, Jim saw that two he had taken for boys were girls about Linda's age, and, like her, they carried guns on their hips and Winchesters in scabbards. Jim held back a smile. A wild bunch, he had told Molly Ryan. They were that, all right. He thought of the men who had stood more than a century before at Lexington with muskets in their hands. They had been called wild, too. Rebels. Even worse names. But what they had done that day had changed the history of the world.

"We don't savvy this," a man behind Linda said. "We allowed you was on Klein's side."

"You're wrong," Jim said. "Linda was wrong. So was Chinook. You make a hell of a bad mistake when you figure that any man who don't live on the mesa is somebody you've got to watch out for."

"We were sure wrong on this huckleberry," Chinook agreed. "You should'a' seen the way he came helling in here, lead cracking all around him. He saved my hide, that's sure."

"We're wasting time!" a man yelled. "Let's ride that bunch down. We'll burn K Cross. . . ."

"No," Jim said sharply. "That's what Klein wants you to try. There may come a day when we'll have to do it, but this ain't

109

the day. I've got a hunch I aim to play. Bill Gray's killing and them cows slaughtered at the ford mean something if we can add it up right."

"Start adding," the man said ominously.

"I ain't got enough figures yet, but I've got enough to know that somebody else is horning into this deal. If we jump the gun like they want us to, I won't get the dead-wood on 'em."

"Maybe you are stringing with Klein," the man muttered angrily. "Sounds like it."

"You say that once more and I'll beat a few teeth down your throat," Jim said. "I'm the law, and I don't aim for you to start breaking it so I have to go after you. One of these days I'll need you men for deputies. Now stay in line till the right day comes."

He swung to the barn and, leading his horse out, mounted. He heard the talk, low-voiced and ominous. This was dynamite on a short fuse. Nobody except their own leaders had ever told these people what to do. There was no school here, no church, no store, or post office. Few of them visited Harmony more than once a year, and, if an outsider ventured across a ford at Gray's Crossing, he was received with sullen hostility.

Howdy Gale had held his position as pack

leader because he bragged that he could lick any man on the mesa, and he received all challenges with such enthusiasm that his reputation as a brutal fighting man had spread over Wild Horse range. Jim could not guess where Howdy was tonight, but his absence was a deciding factor in swinging these people Jim's way.

When Jim rode up, Linda said evenly: "All right, Jim, we're stringing along with you, but if you're lying to us, you're a dead man."

"Fair enough," Jim said. "Looks like I'll live to be a hundred."

"Jake," Linda motioned to one of the boys, "the sheriff's pack horse is in the aspens above the Gray cabin. Fetch him to our place. Lafe, Jap, Mack, you boys stay here till sunup. Come morning, we'll build up another brush pile on Coyote Rock."

"That bunch won't be back," Jim said.

"Won't take no chances." She paused, eyes fixed on Jim. "You can come home with me tonight if you're not afraid."

Somebody laughed. "He oughta be afraid. Howdy ain't gonna like tonight's doings."

"Hell, Jim Bruce ain't afraid of nothing," Chinook growled. "I seen him fight tonight. He'll kill Howdy, Linda."

111

"That'll be worth seeing," Linda said, her voice expressionless as if she had no real interest either way. "Come on, Jim."

There was no talk as they followed the narrow trail back to the main road and turned toward the Gale place. When he had been here before election, he had tried to break down the clannishness of these people, but he had failed. He would succeed this time, or he would die. Linda had left no doubt of his position.

Jim understood how Linda and the rest of them had reasoned. If he rode back across the ford, he was finished. If he stayed, he would fight Howdy. Not because there was anything personal that called for fighting, but because Jim had given an order and been obeyed, and Howdy would consider that a challenge to his authority.

The Gale cabin was dark when they reined up. Linda found a lantern and lighted it. She said: "Take care of the horses. I'll rustle some grub."

When Jim entered the cabin a few minutes later, Linda had started a fire and was frying bacon. As he built a smoke, idling with a shoulder against a doorjamb, he was surprised to find that Linda was as much at home over a stove as she was on a horse or with a gun in her hand.

Without thinking, he said: "You're the damnedest girl."

She swung around, demanding: "Now just what do you mean by that?"

Her man's shirt made a snug fit over her breasts; he found himself wondering what she would look like in a dress. She stood with an egg in her hand, scowling, her eyes pinned on him, and he knew it would take very little to make her lose her temper.

"I never saw you acting like a woman before," he said quickly. "When I was up here before election, we just rode around seeing folks, but dog-goned if you ain't as handy inside the house as outside."

She smiled, good humor flowing across her tanned face. "I thought you meant something else, Jim. The trouble is, I'm not used to being around a civilized man. The ones I'm with most of the time need a quirt or a gun to keep them in line, so I've learned to use both." Turning back, she broke the egg into the frying pan. "Someday I'm going to act like a woman. You'll see."

She set food on the table, moody now, and Jim was silent, sensing the discontent that was in her, the conflict between the life she had been forced to live and the life she wanted.

Jim ate ravenously, and was ashamed

when he admitted he was still hungry and Linda had to fry two more eggs for him. When he was done, he leaned back and rolled a cigarette. He said: "Next time you're in town I'll pay you for supper by buying you a dress. I'll bet you don't even own one."

Temper was bright in her eyes again. "Oh, yes, I do. I'll put it on if. . . ."

"Never mind." He grinned. "You know, Linda, you're a damned good-looking woman. With a dress on and a little fussing with your hair, you'd be downright pretty."

She eyed him suspiciously, as if wondering whether he was rawhiding her, then she rose and began washing dishes. He watched her, thinking of Dobe and Molly Ryan, and telling himself again that there was nothing between Dobe and Linda. She was about Molly's age, but in every other way they were entirely different. Linda belonged to the mountains; she possessed their ageless maturity and primitive beauty, their wildness and their strength.

Jim remained at the table, eyes on Linda's slender back, savoring the intimacy of this moment. For these few minutes he was relaxed and at peace, and it struck him with startling sharpness that he had not felt this way when Angela Klein had been with him the evening before. The distrust he'd felt of her had not been entirely due to the fact that she was Holt Klein's wife, but it had stemmed largely from the driving selfishness that he had sensed in her. Linda, he thought, was neither subtle nor selfish, and it was this quality of forthright honesty that had made him respect her from the first day he had seen her.

Rising, Jim walked to the door and flipped his cigarette stub into the dust, feeling a sudden rush of dissatisfaction. Actually he had had no time for women. He thought of his Spartan life on Pitchfork after his folks had died, of his soul-deep disappointment when he had been forced to sell his cattle to pay George Waldron, of the year he'd spent packing the star, a year of living on top of a volcano that might erupt any time.

He turned to find Linda looking at him. For a moment their eyes locked, a half smile on her full, strong lips, and it struck him then that here was a woman who would not care what sort of volcano a man was sitting on, if she loved him. He started toward her, wanting to tell her how he felt, to tell her that he had kept this feeling buried in the back of his heart from the time she had been his guide before election.

Linda turned away, the smile fading from

her lips, her face tightening under the pressure of her own emotions. She must have sensed what was in his mind, for she walked to her bunk at the other end of the big room. He stopped, uncertain now, feeling that she didn't want to hear what he had intended to say.

For a moment he was puzzled and hurt, wondering if he had been mistaken in thinking she felt about him as he did about her, and if she had cherished the few days they had spent together more than a year ago. Perhaps it had just been a job Howdy had assigned to her. He did not like the thought, but it clung in his mind, the sense of intimacy gone. Now they were strangers, a wall between them.

"I'm going to bed." She sat down on her bunk and pulled off a boot. "You can sleep in Howdy's bunk." She motioned to it. "He won't be back until morning. The kids are with him."

"I'd better sleep in the barn," he said.

She looked at him, indignant. "Don't be silly. If you were any other man, I'd send you packing, but if I can't trust Jim Bruce, I can't trust anybody." She pulled off the other boot, wiggling her toes in the luxury of freedom, her head turned so that he could see only one side of her face. She was being feminine now, a challenging half smile curling the corners of her mouth. "Blow out the lamp and climb in. You need sleep if you're going to lick Howdy tomorrow."

She started unbuttoning her shirt, entirely unconcerned, as if the thought of not trusting him had never occurred to her. Blowing out the lamp, he moved across the dark room to the bunk, pulled off his boots, and lay down. A faint gleam of moonlight showed her straight figure sitting on the edge of the bed.

"Jim, this fight with Howdy is wrong. He'll kill you."

He lifted himself on an elbow, wishing he could see her face, for he sensed an honest concern in her voice. He said: "Maybe he will, but if I don't try, I might as well get out of the country. I've got to have Howdy's help, and, if I don't get it, I can't whip Klein."

"Is that what you want, Jim, to whip Klein?"

He was silent for a moment, weighing the things that had seemed so important in the past, of going back on Pitchfork and getting square with Klein for Tim Ryan's death. He said finally: "I want more than that, I reckon. Seems like when a man sets himself to do something, he's got to do it."

"I think that's just stupid pride," she said hotly, "if that's all there is to it."

Again he was silent, thinking of what Doc Foster had said in Steele's office, and thinking about Waldron and Delaney and Klein. It seemed that a man builds his standards through the years and he must live by those standards. What would be stupid from some men would not be stupid from others. Like Howdy Gale, who was made in his own peculiar mold. He would admire and respect a man who could beat him, but Klein was the kind who would never be satisfied until he had smashed anyone who stood against him.

"It ain't just pride," he said at last. "There are a lot of things I want, but seems like Klein is between me and all of them."

"What, Jim?"

"I'd like to make this a country where folks can live the way they want to, and I'd like to see the country grow."

"You're thinking about that dam again," she said. "I didn't suppose you were so full of wild dreams."

"There's a lot we don't know about each other, I guess. I was going to say I wanted you, but you didn't cotton to the notion of me telling you. You wouldn't believe it, I reckon."

"Jim," she said in the softest tone he had ever heard her use, "I was afraid to hear it . . . that was all. I guess I was afraid you wouldn't mean it, but now I've heard it and it's crazy, too. You'd do better trying to make a pet out of a she-cougar." She lay down. "Crazy or not, I liked to hear it. Now you go to sleep. You've got to fix Howdy's clock for him tomorrow."

She was silent then, and a moment later he heard the steady rhythm of her breathing, but he did not go to sleep at once. He thought he understood how Linda felt. She wanted him to succeed in what he had set himself to do, and, if that meant whipping Howdy, she wanted Howdy whipped. But still her loyalty would be divided. Tomorrow would not be an easy day for her.

He woke with the sun full in his face from the east window. Then he caught the smell of frying bacon, and he heard Linda say: "You're the laziest thing I ever saw, Jim Bruce. The sun's been up for an hour. If you're not out of there in about six seconds, I'll pour this coffee down your neck."

"I'd rather drink it," he said, and, sitting up, rubbed his eyes.

He remained on the edge of the bunk for a

moment, watching her move quickly from the stove to the table. He pulled on his boots and went outside and washed. When he came in, she said briskly: "Sit down, Sheriff. And I'll tell you something you don't know about yourself. You snore."

"I don't believe it." He yawned. "A man who likes to sleep as well as I do couldn't bother with snoring."

"I noticed you like to sleep, all right," she said tartly.

While they ate, he looked around the room, thinking of something that had not occurred to him the night before. The cabin was clean, yet actually it showed little of a woman's influence. It was a log house, built a generation before by Linda's parents. The cabins on the mesa were much alike, and this was typical of them. Here were the usual guns racked on the wall, the bear skins on the floor, a huge set of elk horns, and one picture, a faded print depicting a cowboy roping a grizzly.

Jim rose the instant they were done, right hand reaching for the makings. He said: "I'll take care of the horses."

She looked up, hesitating, then said in a low voice: "You've still got time to ride out."

"I'll make my try."

"I knew you'd say that. Take off your gun belt, Jim, and leave it in here. And watch out for Howdy's bear hugs. If he can squeeze the wind out of you, he'll get you on the ground and you'll be lucky if he kills you."

"I'll remember," Jim said, and went outside.

He watered and fed the horses, finding his pack animal with the others, and made a quick circle of the corrals. He was not surprised when he found the ashes of a branding fire not more than two days old, and the tracks and droppings of a bunch of calves. Twenty or more, he judged. They had been driven southeast toward the Red Wall.

Then Jim understood Howdy Gale's absence, and doubt grew in him. If Howdy had rustled the calves, and there seemed to be no doubt of it, it was more than likely he had killed Bill Gray and shot Dobe. But worse than that, Linda had lied, or, at best, had not told him all that she knew. He walked back to the cabin, suddenly sick.

They began coming then. By the middle of the morning, it seemed to Jim that every man, woman, and child on the mesa except the Gale boys had crowded into the yard. Jim remained away from them, understanding this. They had come to see a fight

121

just as they'd come to watch someone ride an outlaw horse, but this was more than that. Jim Bruce was the first sheriff in the history of San Marcos County who had had the temerity to challenge Howdy, and these people were hoping he'd be the last.

There was a good deal of betting talk, although old Chinook was the only one who backed Jim. He staked everything he had, down to his saddle and belt gun. Then Linda came out of the house with a hundred dollars in gold that she put on Jim at long odds. It surprised him, and it must have surprised the others, but she held her head high, making no excuses.

From where Jim roosted on the top corral bar, he could see the fine green of the aspens on the lower slopes of the Ramparts as clearly as if they were within reach of his arm. Long strips of spruce ran upward toward the bare granite peaks, and here and there, in protected spots of shade, the snow still clung as if reluctant to admit that winter was gone.

The seemingly level stretches of the mesa lay to the south and east, but Jim knew the flat appearance of the cedar and piñon plain was deceiving. Actually it was cut by innumerable cañons so that a man like Howdy Gale, who knew the country, could find a hundred places within ten miles of here where the calves could be safely hidden. Far beyond the mesa he could see the valley, a vast sweep of sage and grass that had a weird appearance in the shifting heat waves weaving crazily before his eyes.

Someone yelled: "Here they come!" Old Chinook beckoned to Jim. Linda had moved back to the cabin to stand in the shade. She was alone, and only then did Jim understand the extent to which she had separated herself from the rest of the mesa people when she had backed him in the fight.

He crossed the yard to her, saying softly: "You shouldn't have bet on me."

Her eyes touched his, then turned away to watch Howdy and the younger Gale boys ride in. She said: "It'll be all right if you lick him. I hate to think what will happen to us if you don't."

Jim walked away, puzzled by what she had said. The crowd had moved back to the corrals and barn, silent, expectant. Howdy Gale was forking a blaze-faced stallion. He lifted a hand to Jim, a wide grin on his lips.

" 'Morning, Sheriff!" Howdy called. "I hear you're fixed for branding."

Howdy swung down, motioning to his

brothers to take his horse. Jim had seen them only once, the first day he had come to the mesa before election, and both had grown in the year since then. Mart was sixteen, Joe thirteen, and, except for the difference in size and the ragged black beard on Howdy's face, they were exact images of their brother. Howdy moved toward Jim, a raw-boned, long-jawed man with eyes and hair as dark as Linda's.

Jim said: "Take off your gun belt."

Howdy came to a flat-footed stop, surprised. "Why, hell, I ain't fixing to use a gun on a man who fights. . . ."

"Take it off," Jim repeated.

Howdy shrugged. "Sure, if it'll make you feel any better." He unbuckled his gun belt and tossed it to his brother Joe.

"I didn't ask for this fight," Jim said.

Again Howdy's dark face showed surprise. "Well, now, sounded to me like you was begging for it."

"You fight because you like to. I fight because I have to. I've got nothing against you, Howdy."

They stood ten feet apart, a small grin of anticipation tugging at the corners of Howdy's mouth, Jim's features set. Howdy said: "I got nothing against you, neither, bucko. You're the best sheriff this county ever had, which ain't saying much. You shouldn't have come up here and started telling my neighbors what to do, like you done last night. Telling 'em is my job. Savvy?"

"I savvy how it's been." Jim motioned toward the ashes of the branding fire. "It ain't gonna keep on being the same. I'm thinking you know where that bunch of K Cross calves went."

"Now mebbe I do." Howdy's grin widened. "Want me to recollect?"

"You're gonna recollect before I'm done. Right now I want a promise out of you. When the sign's right, I'm gonna ask for some help. Will you give it to me?"

Howdy scratched the back of his neck. "I don't help nobody, bucko. You ought to know that."

"Then you're gonna disappoint your friends, because I ain't fighting. No sense to it. I figured that, if I licked you, you'd give me a hand."

"You lick me, mister, and I'll help you rope the moon." Curiosity stirred in the man's meaty face. "What kind of help do you figger you'll need?"

"I ain't man enough to pull Klein out of K Cross if I get enough on him to arrest him. If your outfit starts after him, I'll have a man-sized war in my bailiwick, and I don't want it."

Somebody yelled in disgust: "Let's go home! We ain't gonna see nothing but a blabbing match."

Howdy stood motionless, his forehead lined in thought. Jim, watching the big man warily, told himself that this was the craziest thing he had ever got into, to have to fight and whip a man to get his help.

Suddenly Howdy threw back his great head and bawled a laugh. "No, Monte, you came to see more'n a blabbing match. The tin star was making a deal which same I'm agreeing to when he licks me." Howdy made a half turn toward the man who had called. "You hear that, Monte? *When* he licks me."

Howdy gave no warning. One moment he was relaxed and laughing, the next he was wheeling back and jumping at Jim with the speed of a striking cougar, both fists hammering at Jim's face. Howdy was the bigger and stronger man; Linda had warned Jim of Howdy's bear hugs. Because that was the way he fought, he naturally expected a smaller opponent to back away from him, so Jim did the opposite. He pivoted and, timing his blow carefully, swung a chopping right to the side of Howdy's head that knocked him flat into the dust.

An expectant yell broke out of the crowd when Howdy made his jump, with only old Chinook's reedy voice cheering Jim. Young Mart Gale bawled: "Bust him, Howdy! Bust hell outta him." Then Howdy went flat and the yells changed to groans except for Chinook's howl of joy.

Again Jim fooled everybody. He didn't boot Howdy as Howdy would have done. He stood over the big man, his fists cocked. Slowly Howdy lifted himself to his hands and knees and shook his big head. Then Jim jumped on his back, swinging rights and lefts to the sides of Howdy's head.

"Want your spurs, Sheriff?" Chinook crowed.

Howdy let out a bawl like a hornet-stung bull, reared up, and went over backward. Jim slid off sideways, tripped and fell, and was on his feet again before Howdy could stomp him.

"Come on, boy," Jim taunted. "Why ain't you fighting?"

But the prodding didn't work. Howdy roared a laugh, black eyes a-shine with the pleasure of it. "All right, tin star. Here's some fighting," and came at Jim again.

It was swing and duck. Pivot. Feint. Play for the opening to Howdy's jaw. There were no rules. Howdy tried to knee him in the crotch and failed. He tried to kick Jim's shins, and Jim caught him by the leg and dumped him. Again he dropped on the big man, fists beating at the bearded face.

Howdy had one eye almost closed, his nose was running a scarlet stream, but still he had not been really hurt. Jim knew that. He was using up his strength without doing anything more disastrous to Howdy than slash his face.

Howdy came up off the ground with a tremendous heave, Jim straddling his middle, feet off the ground. Howdy had both arms around him now, squeezing. This was the very thing that Linda had warned Jim against. He heard her now, her scream piercing the roar of the crowd. "Break out of it, Jim! Break out of it!"

A few seconds more and Jim would be finished. His ribs would cave under this pressure, he couldn't breathe, and at the moment he had lost the power to think coherently. He acted instinctively, left hand grabbing a handful of Howdy's hair. He pried the big head back and swung his right to Howdy's nose. It was already bleeding; now he felt it flatten under his fist.

Howdy cried out involuntarily and released his grip. Jim fell away from him, did a complete somersault, and regained his feet. Red dust was all around them now in a choking cloud. For a moment the crowd was subdued except for Chinook's taunting yells. Howdy stood motionless, breathing hard. He wiped a hand across his face and brought it away covered with blood.

He's a killer now, Jim thought. *He ain't fighting for fun. He's hurt.*

Howdy moved forward, weaving as if he were almost out on his feet. Jim was forced to make a decision then. If Howdy was really hurt, this was the time to finish him. If he wasn't, it was a trap. So Jim waited and Howdy jumped forward, hands reaching for Jim, his only desire to grip and tear and maim.

Howdy was in a crouch, trying for Jim's legs to bring him down, and Jim gave him a knee in a straight-up blow on his battered nose, the *crack* of the blow running out across the yard and bringing an involuntary cry out of one of the watchers. Howdy's head snapped back and he fell face down into the trodden red dust.

"What the hell you waiting for?" Chinook screamed: "Boot him, boy! Damn it, give him the toe of your boot!"

But Jim waited. Howdy was beaten. He came to his feet slowly, as if he were very tired. He wiped his face again with a big hand and stared at the blood and dust with his one good eye. He braced himself there, big feet spread, all his assurance drained out of him.

Jim moved in, knowing this was the time to end it. He dodged a flaying fist that swept out like a club and drove a hard right to Howdy's middle, bringing air out of his lungs in a gusty sigh. Howdy tottered, mouth sprung open, struggling for breath. He didn't raise a defensive fist when Jim cracked him on the point of the chin. He fell, slowly at first like a great pine breaking over a faller's axe, and then spilled out full length, dust raising around him.

"You got him, boy!" Chinook howled. "You got him. He'll never get up. Pay me, you gamblers. Shell out."

For a moment Jim stood staring at the fallen man, suddenly realizing that he was tired and feeling throbs of pain in places where he had not known he had been hit.

Linda screamed: "Look out!"

Jim wheeled, caught the blur of a descending gun barrel, and tried to pull away from it. He was too late. He pitched forward into a hard-running current that carried him out into a black, uncharted sea. He could not hear Linda say with slow deep fury: "If you touch him again, Mart, I'll shoot you."

Chapter Seven

Jim spent a week with the Gales. It was a strange week, a week of miracles. Linda sent young Mart to Harmony for Doc Foster, promising dire punishment if he didn't get the medico back in time, for Jim did not recover consciousness as soon as she thought he should. Besides, Howdy's fist-flattened nose needed attention. So when Jim stirred and opened his eyes, he found the pudgy little medico sitting beside his bed.

"Everything's fine," Foster said. "I hear you gave Howdy a hell of a beating. Now you go on back to sleep."

When Jim had dropped off, the doctor rose and walked across the room to Linda and Howdy, who stood beside the stove. Howdy's face was half covered with bandages.

"Keep him quiet," Foster said. "You never know about a head blow like that."

Foster had a patient with a broken leg who lived near the Red Wall. While he was there, a neighbor woman sent for him to look at her croupy baby, so it was the end of the week before he returned to the Gale place. Jim was sitting in front of the cabin, smoking, very much himself again except that he was several pounds thinner than he had been the week before.

The sun, half hidden by the Ramparts, threw a slanted scarlet light upon him. He pulled his hat down over his eyes and lifted a hand in greeting. "Howdy, Doc. Seems like I remember you. Or was it another nightmare?"

Foster swung down, relief mirrored on his round, pale-cheeked face. "Now hold on. Don't tell me I'm that ugly. I may scare babies when they look at me, but, hell, you're a big boy."

Jim laughed. "You look damned good. Linda said you was worried some about me. You can do your worrying over somebody else now. I guess I've just got a thick skull."

Foster reached for Jim's wrist and stood in silence for a moment, then dropped his hand. "Never felt a better pulse. Your skull ain't just thick, my friend . . . must be solid bone. A man should die from a crack like you got."

"How was Dobe when you left town?"

"Aw, he was all right. Molly's nursing him like he was a brother. Or like she was in love with him, which maybe she is. Anyhow, he'll be as good as ever in a few days."

Young Joe Gale came out of the barn and took the doctor's horse, calling: "I'll water and feed him for you, Doc!"

"Thanks, sonny." Foster lowered his voice. "Feel like talking, Jim?"

"Sure."

"I've been around the mesa since I left here. Reckon I'm the only flatlander in the county who can ride through the service berry and scrub oak without getting shot at. These folks talk to me like I was one of 'em."

"They know you're their friend, Doc," Jim said. "They don't think anybody else is."

Foster fished into his vest pocket for a match. "Well sir, Jim, it's the damnedest thing, but now they think you're all right. When you licked Howdy, you made yourself a god to these people. They're primitive and kind of child-like, but they're fine folks, too, if you understand them."

"Yeah," Jim agreed somberly. "I never knew how fine. Howdy thinks I'm something great, and Mart's so ashamed he slugged me that he just sits looking at the floor when he's in the house. I guess Linda took his hide right off his back for it."

"Lost his head when he saw what you'd done to Howdy. They've got their own standards for figuring what's right and what's wrong. But once Howdy was down, it was wrong for Mart to crack you."

Jim nodded. "But if I'd been in the K Cross bunkhouse fighting Sam Pruett, for instance, his boys would have ganged up and killed me."

"Sure," Foster agreed. "But take these mesa folks now. They remind me of a bunch of cavemen. Howdy was fighting for his place as top dog, and you challenged him. Now that he ain't top dog, he'll go along with you."

"I reckon so," Jim said. "That's what I was fighting for."

Foster lighted his pipe and pulled hard for a moment, his eyes on the scarlet sky above the Ramparts. He asked: "What are you aiming to do now, Jim?"

"I want to have a talk with Howdy. He got away with Klein's calves. Then I thought I'd pay Klein a visit."

Foster took the pipe out of his mouth. He said in disgust: "Damned if they ain't been feeding you loco weed."

"Not lately. I've got a hunch, Doc, and I'm going to play it."

Foster puffed for a moment. "Jim, I've lived on Wild Horse River for more'n twenty years. Got here right after the Utes

134

were moved out. Now, I haven't made much money. Haven't wanted to. I like the country and I like most of the people, so I've had what I wanted . . . just like Klein, for instance, has got what he wanted."

"Hell of a lot of difference," Jim grunted. "You're satisfied and he ain't and never will be."

Foster took his pipe out of his mouth and stared unseeingly at the blackened bowl. "I'm taking a long time to say what I've got on my mind. Maybe you never thought of it, but a doctor knows things he's got no business telling. He's got a set of ethics like a lawyer. Or a priest."

Jim flipped his cigarette into the dust and waited. He had never heard the medico talk like this before, and he sensed that Foster had something important to say and was finding it difficult to put it into words.

"I'm going to tell you some things anyhow," Foster went on. "Might help you get it added up. Take finding that obsidian under Bill Gray's head. I got to thinking. Steele and Smoke Malone are as close as that." He held up two fingers pressed together. "You know how it is with me, traveling all times of night and day whenever some kid gets the sniffles or whatever. Well, I've seen them two together on horses.

135

Mostly close to the river somewhere. And I've seen Malone sneak into Steele's office when decent folks were in bed and asleep."

Jim rolled another smoke, glancing obliquely at the doctor. He said: "I don't think Malone killed Gray and shot Dobe."

Foster shrugged. "Maybe not. Now here's the other thing. I've brought all of Waldron's children into this world of shame and sorrow. Four of 'em, mind you, and his wife damned near died the last time. And Delaney" — Foster shook his head — "had typhoid last winter and he'd be pushing up the daisies right now if I hadn't camped right beside his bed for forty-eight hours straight hand running."

The doctor knocked his pipe against his boot heel, his face filled with misery. "They came to my house that night after you left town. Just Delaney and Waldron. Told me to get out of town *pronto*. Said you wouldn't last bucking Klein, and, if I was gonna side with you, they aimed to see I sloped out of the country."

"The hell."

Foster rose. "I've got to get back to town. Been gone too long now."

"Stay here tonight."

"Can't do it. Missus Starbuck's baby is about due. I ain't worried about Waldron

136

and Delaney. Don't get that notion." He looked down at Jim, a deep bitterness working in him. "It's just that we've all got to have something to live for. My job is curing sick folks, or fixing it so they can die a little easier. Gives me some satisfaction, even it don't make me rich. Like Klein wanting more cows and more land and more money. And you wanting to see justice done and get back on Pitchfork. But what in hell is wrong with Waldron and Delaney?"

Jim stared at the doctor, the unlit cigarette still in his hand, knowing that Foster had bared his soul and showed the depth of his hurt, something he had probably never done to anyone else in San Marcos County, this man who had brought physical and moral comfort to so many. Underneath his brusqueness, Foster was a sensitive man who took more of his pay in gratitude than he did in money, and now Jim felt totally inadequate to say the things that should be said.

"I don't know what's wrong with 'em, Doc," Jim said. "All I've got to say is that they're a disgrace to the human race. They're crazy, too, or they'd remember that they might be needing a doctor someday."

"I thought about that, too," Foster said morosely. "Well, I've got to ride."

Jim rose, lighted his cigarette, and walked with the doctor to the barn. He said: "Strikes me they're getting at me through you. Maybe they think you're the only friend I've got, and, with you gone, I'd cave."

"But they don't love Klein no more than we do. It don't make much sense."

"It would if we knew everything. Might be something big, Doc, so big they'd rather do anything than to let it slip out of their reach."

"Hell, they're doing all right." Foster said nothing more until they reached the barn. Then he called: "Joe, fetch my horse out, will you?"

A moment later the boy led the doctor's horse out of the barn, and Foster stepped into the saddle. "Don't get into no more tussles, Jim."

"I don't aim to." Jim walked back to the house, Foster holding his horse down to match Jim's pace. "Thanks for coming out, Doc."

"Glad to. Just stay alive, boy." He reined up and stared down at Jim, an unexplained worry still working in him. "I'm just a gossipy old woman, but I've got to say one more thing. Stay away from Angela. She'll make a fool out of you just like she's doing with George Waldron."

Jim frowned, wondering if this was just a wild guess on Foster's part, or whether he knew about Angela's coming out to Pitchfork and about him stopping in the woman's room that morning before he had left town.

"Make yourself plain, Doc," Jim said, tight-lipped.

"Aw hell," Foster said, abashed now, "that was one thing I didn't aim to tell you. I can't prove nothing. So long."

Whirling his horse, Foster rode out of the clearing and a moment later disappeared into the scrub oak. Jim was still standing there, staring after him, wondering what he had meant about Angela's making a fool out of George Waldron, when Linda rode in from the west. She dismounted and handed the reins to Joe, watching Jim curiously. She said nothing until she was close enough to touch Jim. She cleared her throat, and Jim, only then aware of another's presence, wheeled, his hand whipping down to gun butt.

The girl stepped back, surprised. "I thought you knew I was here. I didn't aim to scare you."

Jim lowered his gaze, ashamed. "I was a million miles away, I guess. Doc was here. He says I'm all right."

"I'm glad." She frowned. "But I wanted to see him."

"He couldn't stay."

She turned toward the house, calling back: "Get some wood for me, will you, Jim? I'll start supper."

Howdy and Mart rode in a few minutes later, but it was not until after supper and the boys had gone to bed in the barn that Jim asked the question he had known from the first he must ask.

"I'm riding out in the morning, Howdy, and I've got to find out one thing before I go. Did you steal them calves?"

Howdy's dark face was lighted by a wide grin. "I knowed you'd get around to that sooner or later. No, sir, I didn't. I bought 'em cheap, no questions asked."

Linda came from the stove where she had been washing dishes and sat down at the table beside Jim. She said: "You might as well know all of it. We haven't been exactly honest, but we aren't crooks, either. It goes back to the time the folks first came here. They could have settled in the valley, but they liked it up here. They got along for a while, then they had a bad year and went to town to get a loan. Waldron turned them down. Then they went to Delaney and he said no credit."

140

"I remember how it was," Howdy said somberly. "Linda was too young. She's just heard us talk about it, but I remember. I was old enough to tag along with Pappy. I stood there in the store staring at them jars of horehound and such that Delaney had, my mouth a-watering. Then they got to yelling at each other and I forgot about the candy. I thought they was gonna start their guns talking afore Pappy walked out."

Jim nodded. He had never heard it before, but it was like Waldron and Delaney, and it explained a good many things about the mesa people. He said: "They're nickel-nursers, all right."

"After that, Pappy said to hell with Harmony," Linda went on. "He said we'd stay right here and live off venison and somebody else's beef, if it came to that. The other families looked up to Pappy just like they look up to Howdy now, and they strung along. Since then we've all been living by ourselves and buying stolen property and helping outlaws get through the mountains to Utah and not caring what the sheriffs in Harmony thought."

"Now you've got the truth," Howdy inserted. "That was why us folks don't take to outsiders, especially lawmen. But we voted for you 'cause we figgered you was made of

141

different stuff. Reckon you are, too."
Howdy felt gingerly of his nose. "Mister, I'd
think that licking you gave me was just a bad
dream if this thing didn't hurt like a boil."

Jim leaned across the table. "Howdy,
have you got a bill of sale for them calves?"

"You damn betcha. Me 'n' the kids
moved the calves 'cause we knew it'd save
trouble. You'd mess around and Klein
might come looking for 'em, but it was a
square enough deal."

Howdy fished a dirty scrap of paper from
his pocket and handed it to Jim. It was a bill
of sale all right, much like any other bill of
sale except for one thing. The difference
was so startling that Jim sat there for a long
moment, staring at the signature, forgetting
to breathe. It had been signed by Sam
Pruett.

Jim laid the paper on the table, his face
wiped clean of expression. "I don't get this,
Howdy. Pruett was in Harmony that night
with Klein and his wife. Leastwise, he was
there mighty early the next morning."

Howdy shrugged. "Dunno about that. I
didn't see him out here. Didn't even see his
boys shoot them cows. Me and Mart and
Joe were on the mesa, waiting for 'em. We
heard the shooting 'bout two, three in the
morning. Purty soon Yank Beeman and

Zane Wheeler drove those calves up to where we was waiting. Beeman gave me the bill of sale and said to keep my mug shut. Said Pruett would have some more if I kept mum."

Howdy Gale had more than his share of faults, but Jim didn't think that lying was one of them. He was silent for a time, thinking about what Howdy had said and feeling like a man trying to grip a handful of fog. These things he had seen and heard since he had talked to Angela more than a week before must make a pattern, but to him they were still only odd pieces of a puzzle that did not fit.

"Strikes me," Jim said at last, "that Klein didn't have nothing to do with it. I thought at first he'd slaughtered his own cows and drove his calves onto the mesa just to make me think you folks did it. Then he figured I'd come up here and arrest somebody and get shot trying it."

"Yeah, could be that way," Howdy agreed. "He's been wanting to ride in here and clean us out, and that'd give him all the excuse he'd need."

Jim shook his head. "But I don't think it's that way. Looks like somebody's promoting a war, or them cows wouldn't have been killed right there on the river. If they just wanted to make some mavericks, they'd have done the job back in the aspens."

"Looks like Klein to me," Howdy grunted.

"Don't stand to reason," Jim said doggedly. "It's my guess somebody is using me and you folks to get at Klein, somebody who wants him dead, and they're hoping that one of us will do the job without anybody suspicioning them."

"What are you fixing to do now?" Howdy demanded. "Arrest me?"

"Hell, no. I aim to go see Klein. He'd like to see this bill of sale." Jim picked it up. "Can I have it?"

"No." Linda rose, a hand going up to her throat, the most feminine gesture Jim had ever seen her make. "You're out of your mind, Jim. Doc told us about you and Klein. He'd rub you out as soon as anybody else, or sooner."

"Yeah, and he'd fix it so nobody'd be the wiser," Howdy said. "Wouldn't be smart, Jim."

"It's the only way to shove this thing into the open." Jim tapped the bill of sale. "This looks like Pruett's writing. If it is, and if Klein didn't have nothing to do with it, we'll have fireworks soon as Klein sees it."

"You can take the bill of sale," Howdy

said uneasily, "but if you walk into K Cross, it'd be about as smart as going hunting for grizzlies with a pea-shooter."

Linda was still staring at Jim, paler than he had ever seen her. She said: "You're stubborn, Jim, and you're foolish. Isn't there anything we can say that will change your mind?"

"No."

Without a word she turned and walked to her bunk.

Howdy winked at Jim and snorted: "Women!"

Jim woke in the morning to see young Mart building a fire. When Mart saw that Jim was awake, he said: "Linda's out on her horse. You want to get breakfast?"

Jim nodded, puzzled by the girl's absence. "Sure, I'll get it."

After Mart had gone back to the barn, Jim wondered what would take Linda riding in the night and why she would be gone at a time when he was ready to leave. He had not told her he loved her, but he thought she knew. If she did, she must have gone away to avoid hearing him tell her.

Now, as he made his coffee and sliced ham, he told himself that Linda must like him. She would not have bet on him in his fight with Howdy if she had not, nor would she have been so concerned about his going to K Cross. Before he had regained his strength, she had cared for him with the same tenderness that Molly Ryan had shown Dobe Jackson.

Still, it did not mean she loved him. Or it might be that her family ties were too strong to be broken for any man. He remembered what she had said about being a he-woman and patching her brother's duds and cooking their meals. Then the first night here in the cabin, he remembered how she had been both inviting and perversely cool; he had told her he wanted her and she'd said it was crazy, that he'd do better to make a pet out of a she-cougar.

He had planned to tell Linda how he felt before he left. Well, he wouldn't be telling her anything now. Perhaps it was just as well she was gone. It wouldn't work, not for the two of them, Linda coming from the mesa and Jim from the valley. Linda's man should come from the mesa; he should be the kind who held to the same tough ways the Gales did. Then he realized he was only making excuses for her. He would have liked to have told her good bye, to thank her for what she had done for him.

He did not tell Howdy how he felt, and he

carefully masked the bitterness that Linda's absence raised in him. After breakfast he packed the few things in the cabin that belonged to him. All of them carefully avoided Linda in their talk.

Jim shook hands with young Joe, who had brought his saddled horse from the barn, then with Mart, who mumbled: "Sorry I slugged you, Sheriff."

"It's all right, Mart," Jim said. "I'll gamble you won't do it again."

"Hell, he just never saw me on my back before," Howdy said. "Lost his head, that's all."

Jim held out his hand to the big man. "I don't want to fight you again."

"I'm the one who don't want that fight." Howdy pointed to his nose. "You sure made a mess out of it. First fight I ever had I didn't get no fun out of."

"We made a deal. Remember?"

Howdy was indignant. "Sure I remember. We've got brush piled up on Coyote Rock again. You get word to us you need us, and we'll fire that brush. We'll have twenty guns for you." He scratched the back of his hairy neck, dark eyes showing his concern. "How 'bout me riding with you today, Sheriff?"

Jim stepped into the saddle. "The sign ain't right yet. Howdy, I've got a hunch that by sundown I'll know some things that'll open our eyes a foot wide. Then I'll need you and I'll get word to you."

"But damn it, Klein will gun you down the minute you show up on K Cross range."

"Not if I can show him that bill of sale first. Howdy, I want you to tell Linda that I. . . ."

"I won't tell Linda nothing," Howdy broke in, dark face suddenly ugly. "She made her bed, and, damn her, she's gonna lie in it. You tell her yourself."

Jim did not understand what the big man meant, but he did not feel like asking questions. He said — "So long." — and left the clearing. For a time he rode through close-growing scrub oak, taking the trail to Gray's Crossing, then he reached a small park and reined up, staring out across the mesa. There was no wind this morning, and there was no sign of life in this primitive world except a few pillars of smoke rising from cabins hidden in the brush.

He went on, the sun crawling up into a cloudy sky. Shadows ran across the land as a cloud hid the sun, then they were gone and the morning light was sharp upon the vast sweep of the mesa. He was in the brush again; he rounded a turn in the trail and pulled up at once. Linda sat her saddle directly in front of him, her breasts rising and falling with her breathing, her tanned face quite pale.

"I've been waiting for you," she said.

Jim understood then what Howdy had meant and why the man had been angry when he had mentioned Linda's name. She had cut her ties, the only ties she'd had in a life that had been hemmed in by the restrictions of her people, and now she would go with him wherever he went. At first a fine glow ran through him, for this was what he wanted more than anything else, then he remembered the job that lay before him. He might be dead before the day was gone.

"I'm glad you did," he said. "I wanted to tell you good bye, and to thank you. . . ."

"You're not telling me good bye, Jim." Her lips were tight against her teeth; one hand clutched the saddle horn, knuckles white. "You'll need me at K Cross. I'm going with you."

"I want you to go with me," he said, "but not today. This is a job I've got to do myself. There's a good chance I won't leave K Cross alive."

"That's why I'm going with you, Jim!" she cried. "Why do you think I left home? Why . . . ?" She stopped, suspicion flowing through her. "That first night you told me you wanted me. I said I didn't want to hear it unless you meant it. If you didn't, I'll kill you and myself, too."

He looked intently at her, watching her face that had been soft with her feeling for him and then was suddenly hardened by the thought he had not meant what he had said. He understood how she felt. What she had said about killing would have been an empty threat from any woman except Linda Gale, who had been raised on the mesa and who had been taught that violence is the final law.

"I'm going to tell you something I've been putting off," he said. "I meant what I said that night. I love you. There were a lot of things that night we didn't know about each other, but we know them now. You're the kind of woman a man would be proud to have for a wife. When this is over, I want to marry you, if you'll have me."

"Today, Jim. Of course, I'll have you. We won't wait until this is over."

"No." He said it gently, hoping that she would understand.

"Let the trouble go, Jim!" she cried wildly. "It's not worth dying over."

"And have you hate me because I was afraid to do what had to be done." He shook his head. "You wouldn't love a man you couldn't respect. And I'd hate myself. I'll play my hand out, Linda. Tomorrow, if I'm lucky. . . ."

"Lucky!" She stared at him, angry, bitter. "You're just like Howdy, and I thought you were different. All you know is to fight, but you don't really want to fight. You think you've got to do what other people expect you to do."

She straightened, a hand lifting the reins, her face twisted by the rage that ran through her like a consuming flame. "All right, Jim, if that's the way you want it. Now I'll tell you what I told Howdy. I'm done with living this way . . . like a bunch of Utes. I'm going to be a woman, Jim. If I'm not yours, I'll be some other man's, and you can blame yourself."

She dug in her spurs and swept past him, the red mesa dust rolling up behind her. He hipped around in the saddle to watch her, knowing he had been right and still regretting that she had taken it this way. It was as if he had been drained of all emotion, of all hope. He knew how proud she was; he knew the strength of her will. She had meant exactly what she had said.

Then she was gone from his sight, hidden in the scrub oak. The dust was all that remained to remind him she had been here.

He went on, and an hour later crossed the river. The carcasses of the slaughtered cattle were still there, the stench of a choking stink in his nostrils. He saw Bill Gray's boat, tied to a willow just above the fast water of the gorge. He saw these things and yet he didn't see them, for his thoughts were fixed on Linda.

Chapter Eight

After he was across Wild Horse River, Jim swung his horse toward the foothills of the Ramparts. He stopped at noon to cook a meal, the K Cross buildings still more than an hour's ride, and afterward he took time to smoke a cigarette. There was no need to hurry. He may have been seen, but he doubted that it made any difference. Holt Klein, smart in many ways, was stupid in others. Arrogantly proud, he would not foresee that any enemy would have the temerity to ride in alone as Jim was doing now.

From where Jim lingered in the lower fringe of the aspens, the valley fell away to the north and east. It held a rich carpet of grass, marked by the sharp green of willows that hugged the banks of the small streams that came down from the Ramparts to meander across the flat to Wild Horse River. Doc Foster had called it right when he'd said that Klein wanted more land and more cattle and more money. With him, every decision was a matter of expediency, and doubts of his own wisdom entered Jim's mind.

It was possible that Jim could drive a wedge between Klein and Pruett with the bill of sale Howdy had given him, but he would not change Klein, who would never give up his goal of driving the Gales and Chinook and the others off Banjo Mesa. He would be diverted for the moment, but not for long. Thinking about it now as he nursed his cigarette, Jim knew he could not change his plan. At least, he would find out who was back of Gray's murder and Dobe's shooting.

Klein had built K Cross slowly through the years, beginning after his marriage to Angela. His tools had been murder and robbery and threats, just as Angela had said that night in Jim's cabin. Now, tossing his cigarette into the coals, another thought struck Jim. Why had Klein been just another rancher in the valley until his marriage, then, after that, he had set out to build the empire that was K Cross? Jim kicked out his fire, logic forcing an answer upon him. Angela had set flame to the man's inherent ambition, and in that way she had become responsible for making Klein the man he was.

Mounting, Jim's eyes swept the valley again, thinking how Klein's crimes had piled one upon the other, that K Cross range was watered by the blood and fertilized by the dead dreams of little men, who, like Tim Ryan and the mesa people, wanted only to be let alone.

Far to the south, beyond Jim's range of vision, San Marcos Creek meandered across the valley, a shallow stream flowing between high banks toward the river. The good soil lay on this side, a rock-strewn desert on the other. Out there were the little ranches, the ten-cow outfits that would never be anything else because they had only the leavings, the hardscrabble that Klein did not want.

Jim rode on, wondering about Angela and whether the poverty of childhood had had anything to do with Klein's actions during the past twelve years. He came presently to the K Cross buildings, riding in slowly and seeing no sign of life. Everything here contributed to the appearance of wealth and strength that Holt Klein wanted his ranch to have.

The rambling, two-story house was built of stone, the barns, bunkhouse, cook shack, and other buildings were frame and painted white, the corrals were strong and well-kept. But there was no fence around the house, no trees, no flowers, no lawn. It was a man's ranch built for men. A stranger riding by would not guess that a woman lived here, a beautiful woman who had failed to make an impression on the appearance of her husband's ranch.

Jim swung down and tied, wondering if anyone was home. He was still standing there at the hitch pole when a man stepped out of the bunkhouse, a cocked gun in his hand, and moved warily toward Jim. He asked truculently: "Whatta you want, tin star?" It was Yank Beeman who had given Howdy Gale the bill of sale for the calves.

"Holt," Jim said. "Where is he?"

Beeman was a big man, typical of the salty hands who rode for Klein. He had come to the valley about the time Sam Pruett had, a fact that was also true with Zane Wheeler, who had helped Beeman deliver the calves, and Red Landers, who had died in Chinook's barn the night of the raid.

Beeman moved forward, boot heels stirring the dust. He said: "Good thing for you, Holt ain't here. He'd shoot you the minute he got sight of your ugly mug."

"Maybe not," Jim said. "I've got news that might change his mind."

Beeman's lips pulled away from brown teeth in a taunting grin. "I don't reckon anything will change his mind. Not as far as you're concerned. Now get on that roan and get to hell out of here."

"You've got sight of my ugly mug," Jim said. "Why don't *you* shoot me?"

Beeman glanced at the house and licked his lips. "I ain't got no such orders."

"Yank, who is it?"

It was Angela calling from the front door. Jim made a half turn so he could see her and still watch Beeman. She was wearing a new wine-colored dress, one that she had bought, Jim thought, in Delaney's Mercantile the last time she had been in Harmony. Beeman shifted his weight, swearing bitterly, and stood staring sullenly at Angela, ignoring her question.

Angela came across the porch, a slim and shapely woman who seemed entirely out of place here. She raised a hand to shade her eyes, then saw who it was and cried: "Jim! I didn't know it was you. Yank Beeman, put that gun up. Come in, Jim."

"Holt, he don't want nobody like this here star-toter . . . ," Beeman began.

"I'll take the responsibility," Angela said irritably. "Come in, Jim."

"Petticoat rule, Yank," Jim said softly, and walked to the house, giving Beeman his back.

"It's nice of you to call, Jim." Angela held out her hand. "I don't know what's the matter with Beeman. He thinks he's a watchdog, I guess. When Holt's gone, he insists on leaving Beeman here, but he isn't my choice. There are a lot of men I'd rather have around than Yank."

She led him into the huge front room with its cavernous stone fireplace across the north end. It was exactly the sort of living room Jim would have expected to find in Klein's house — with massive walnut furniture and bear skins on the floor and Navajo blankets thrown carelessly across a leather couch.

There was a lamp with a smoke-blackened chimney on the big table in the middle of the room; there were a few battered magazines and papers around it. A saddle had been dumped in a corner by the fireplace, a half-dozen rifles were leaning against the wall beside it. The combined smells of tobacco and sweat and whiskey lingered in the room.

Angela stood in the doorway, an angry frown still on her face. "He makes me so damned mad, Jim," she said loudly. "It isn't any wonder I don't have a friend on this range with a big ape like that standing out there."

Beeman had followed. Now he stopped in front of the porch. Jim looked past Angela at the man who was glaring at her back; then Angela slammed the door, and it seemed to Jim that she was making too much show of her anger. He couldn't tell whether it was real or phony, but it could have been real.

The frown fled from Angela's face and she smiled. "I'm sorry, Jim, but no matter who came to see me, it would be this way." She gestured wearily. "It's part of what I tried to tell you the other night. I've got to get out of here . . . I'll go crazy if I don't."

"I can see how it would be," he said, and remembered what Doc Foster had said about Angela and George Waldron. It was not a situation he liked any better than he had liked finding her in his cabin that night. "I wanted to see Holt."

"That's all right to tell Yank Beeman," she said, "but not me."

Jim reached for the makings and rolled a smoke. "No, I'm really here to see Holt. This is business, not pleasure like we were talking about."

"Pleasure!" She laughed lightly. "Well, it would be pleasure to have a man around who didn't look at me like . . . like a stallion looks at a mare." She got red in the face then. "I'm sorry, Jim. Holt won't be back till dark. You can see him then, although I don't think he'll want to talk business with you. But whether you wait or not, I want you to see the female part of the house."

She led him down a hall to her room in the back. He knew that this was dangerous, but it would make her angry if he didn't go and he would lose any chance he had of securing her help in putting a rope on Klein's neck.

She opened a door at the end of the hall and stepped aside for him. It was a pleasant room with two windows through which she could look out upon the Ramparts. She had made pink organdy curtains for the windows. There was a rosewood bed that was covered with an expensive lace spread, a bureau, and a wardrobe lined with bird's eye maple.

"Like it?" Angela asked.

"Sure I like it. Ain't much like the front of the house."

"No, it isn't," she agreed. "This is one thing he has done for me. I suppose it's the most comfortable prison a woman ever had, but it's still a prison, Jim. This is the only room in the house that I can call mine." She motioned to a velvet-covered love seat. "Sit down. I'll get some coffee."

She whirled away, her skirt molding the round curves of hips and thighs. He heard her heels tap along the hall, then a door closed, and there was no sound for several moments. Jim smoked his cigarette down and put it out, moving idly about the room. For a time he stood at a window. Yank Beeman was not in sight, and he wondered where the man had gone and what he was thinking.

Jim sat down on the love seat and rolled another cigarette. Somehow, things didn't quite jibe. The talk about Klein being niggardly with his wife was not true as far as the room was concerned. Her expensive furniture undoubtedly had come from Denver, and the cost of getting it here must have been considerable.

She came in with a tray of coffee, cups, and saucers, and small cakes covered with white icing.

"I want to prove one thing to you, Jim," Angela said. "I am a better cook than that miserable supper I fixed for you the other night would make you think."

"It was all right," he said.

She laughed shortly. "Don't lie just to be polite. You aren't the kind of man who can do it."

"Like Sam Pruett?"

She had started to pour the coffee. Now she paused, eyes pinned on Jim's face as if not quite sure how she should take his words. Then she filled the cups and put the coffee pot down. "Why, yes, Sam is the kind who lies gracefully, but you're not Sam."

"No," Jim said, "I'm not. I reckon there are several things Sam does gracefully."

He rose and, walking to the window, tossed his cigarette through it onto the bare, trodden earth of the yard. When he came back and sat down, she handed him a cup of coffee.

"Some of the boys were in town last night and saw Doc Foster. He said you'd beaten Howdy Gale. That's wonderful, Jim. There isn't another man on Wild Horse River who could have done it."

She said it as if she really thought it was wonderful, but it struck Jim that Angela might be doing a little graceful lying herself. He took a cake and stuffed it into his mouth, his eyes avoiding hers when he said: "It was quite a ruckus, all right."

She had pulled a rocking chair around so that it was directly in front of the love seat. She sat down and leaned forward, her cup and saucer held in front of her.

"Let's be honest with each other, Jim. When I left you that night after I'd been out to your place, I thought I had made a mistake. It's like I told you. A woman should always take the indirect way with a man, but I couldn't with you. It was a chance of a life-

162

time. We'd come to town, and you know that's something we don't do very often. Holt had said you were on the creek and I knew that you'd stop at your place before you came to town. You always do, don't you, Jim?"

Nodding, he took another cake. It struck him as strange that Angela, who claimed to be a prisoner on K Cross, would know that, but both Klein and Pruett were familiar with his habits. Probably one of them had told her.

She smiled and sat back in her chair. "There just wasn't any other chance to contact you, Jim, and let you know how I felt, but you held me off and I thought I'd failed. Then you stood up to Holt the next morning in the hotel and I knew I hadn't failed. I knew it even before you came up to my room."

He took another cake, the uneasiness that he always felt when he was with her tugging at him again. "I can't stay here, Angela. If Holt didn't have an excuse before to shoot me, he would if he found me in your bedroom."

"You can stay here long enough for me to finish what I have to say," she said sharply. "I may never have another chance. You see, Jim, I never felt more wonderful in all my life than when you came to my room. You held me in your arms and you kissed me." A tremulous smile touched her lips. "I had never been kissed like that before. It did something to me to be kissed like that, to know that at least one man could think of me in some other way than just a piece of female flesh."

He rose, finding it hard to breathe. "That was good cake, Angela."

"You aren't going, Jim." She got up and put the coffee cup down. "You aren't going until I'm done. I know how you feel. I'm another man's wife, but you forgot that for one minute. When I look back over my life, I can't think of any other moment when I was as happy as when you held me in your arms and kissed me."

She had moved to the door and put her back to it, hands knotted at her sides, her face very pale. This time, he had told himself, he was not going to touch her, and now he felt a quick surge of panic. He had been afraid of her and he was afraid of her now, more afraid than he was of Klein or Pruett or any man or combination of men on Wild Horse range. He thought of Pruett, and of what Doc Foster had hinted about Angela and George Waldron, and he thought he knew how it could have been with them.

"I came here to see Holt," Jim said in a low voice. "I'll come back when he's here."

She was breathing hard, her hands fisted at her sides. "I won't let you go, Jim. I don't know what you've heard about me and Sam, but it isn't true. It's you, Jim, just you. I know it sounds crazy, and I guess it is, but I think it was because you had the courage to stand against Holt. You showed it when you ran for sheriff and you showed it when you talked that way to him in the hotel dining room." She stepped away from the door. "I won't keep you if you don't want to stay, but you can quit worrying about my being Holt's wife. I'll be a widow before long."

He was free to go, but now he hesitated, wondering what she had meant about being a widow. He said: "You sound pretty sure about that."

"I am sure," she said, her head held high. "You'll kill Holt. You'll have to. Or he'll kill you. That's the real reason I went to see you. I wanted to warn you, but I couldn't find the right words for it. It isn't easy, Jim, trying to say all the things that have to be said."

"I'm a lawman, Angela," he said. "I can't just go out and kill a man and take justice into my own hands. You don't seem to understand that."

"I understand, but you don't understand Holt. You're in his way. You've been in his way before, but now it's personal. He hates you, Jim. He can't stand humiliation, and you've humiliated him in a way that he will never forgive you for. He'll have you bushwhacked, just as he has a dozen other men, if you don't kill him first. I don't think you're the kind of fool who'll wait for a bullet like Tim Ryan got."

"I want proof that he was responsible for Tim's death," Jim said stubbornly. "Then I'll arrest him. I thought I told you that before."

"You are a fool," she said, her voice low and filled with brooding bitterness. "I'm trying to make you see that this isn't just for me. I've got reason to hate him, but it's you I'm thinking about. Even if I could give you the proof, which I can't, arresting him wouldn't do any good. He'd hire the best lawyer in the state and he'd buy his way out of jail."

"Not if I have the evidence I've been looking for," he said. "I'll hang him."

"No, you won't, Jim. You've looked for that evidence for a year and you haven't found it." She came to him and put her hands on his arms. "I suppose I know more about Holt than anyone else, but I've never seen him pay off a man for murder. I've heard horses at midnight. Men have come in, killers, strangers, men I didn't know. I've slipped out of my room and gone down the hall to listen, but I can't swear to anything. I heard the jingle of gold and a word or two, but you know I couldn't go on the witness stand and swear that Holt hired someone to murder Tim Ryan."

"No, I guess you couldn't," he said, "but I'll get my teeth into something, and, when I do, I'll bust him."

"If you live." Her hands tightened on his arms. "I can't go on like this, Jim. Take me with you. I'll live with you. You've got a house. I'll cook your meals and I'll take care of you. I . . . I don't care what people say."

"I wouldn't do that and you know it." He pulled free and moved to the door. "I told you I came here to see Holt. When he finds out about Pruett, things are gonna change fast."

She jumped as if she had been stung. "What about Sam?" she asked.

"He's been stealing calves, not the mesa bunch like Holt thinks. I've got a bill of sale he signed."

"Who gave it to you?"

"Howdy Gale."

"You're sure Sam signed it?"

"I'm sure. I know his writing."

She took a long breath, her lips trembling. "Jim, don't go at it this way. I'm not trying to protect Sam, although he's been good to me. Sam could be on your side. Don't make an enemy out of him." She changed completely now, her sense of certainty gone.

He said: "You told me a while ago that the talk about you and Sam wasn't true. What about you and Waldron?"

He asked it deliberately, hoping to surprise her into making an admission of some sort, but it didn't work. She said, the brooding bitterness in her voice again: "You don't believe anything I've said, do you, Jim?"

"I wouldn't put it that way. I know there's some mighty queer things going on, and I figure you know a hell of a lot more'n you're telling."

"Go on, Jim." She motioned to the door. "I've got down on my knees to you, and this is what I get for it."

He put a hand on the doorknob and turned it, disappointment in him. He sensed that he had come close to the truth, but still he knew no more than he had. He asked: "What's Waldron after?"

"I said you were a fool," she said hotly. "Waldron is older than I am, he's got a wife

168

and four children, and yet you listen to gossip like an old woman."

"What's he after?" Jim asked again.

"The biggest thing that ever hit the western slope," she flared. "Now get out of here before I lose my temper or begin to cry. I don't cry for many men, Jim."

She was proud, and she had failed in what she had tried to do. He knew there was no time to ask anything else. He pulled the door open, eyes on her white bitter face, and even then he could not be sure how much of what she had said was true and how much had been lies. He might be misjudging her. It was possible she had been honestly trying to warn him.

"So long," he said, and turned.

He stopped, flat-footed. Klein stood in the hall, a gun in his hand, a malicious grin on his thin lips. "Well, Sheriff, this is a surprise, but when a man's got a wife like I have, I guess he shouldn't be surprised at anything."

Angela stumbled past Jim into the hall, crying hysterically. "I'm so glad you're here, Holt. I've been scared. . . ."

"Shut up," the big man said. "Looks like you made him real comfortable with cake and everything."

"I had to do it, Holt." She reached him,

her hands out to grip his gun arm.

"Stop your lying." He pushed her aside with his left hand. "You've lied to me too many times. Ain't you ever satisfied?"

"You've never tried to satisfy me," Angela flared. "Cows, cows, cows. That's all you know."

"It's what you wanted when you married me," Klein said bitterly. "I worked like a dog to build K Cross . . . and for what? Hell, I was better off with five hundred cows and a couple of hands than I am now. Well, a man don't have to keep standing for what I have." He took a long breath, watching Jim. "Take off your gun belt, bucko."

Angela seemed to understand what her husband meant to do, and with that understanding there must have come a realization of her own danger. She jumped at Klein, trying to grab his right arm, screaming: "You can't do it, Holt!"

He struck her with his left hand, knocking her against the wall. Her feet slid out from under her and she lay on the floor, moaning and making no effort to get up.

"You're a brave man," Jim breathed.

"I'm a careful one," Klein said. "Drop your gun belt. I never kill a man in front of my wife."

Chapter Nine

For a moment Jim stared at Klein, feeling the evil that was in this man. He was both hard and cunning; he played the direct game when it suited him, the devious game when the situation called for it. Now, certain that he held the top hand, he wasted no time in being devious.

Slowly Jim obeyed Klein's order, thinking that everything Angela had said about him was true. Being married to him would be the greatest hell a woman could experience. Jim had no doubt that Angela had meant to double-cross him, that when he had killed Klein she would be done with him, but now, his eyes pinned on Klein's tough, brutal face, he felt more sympathy for the woman than he ever had before.

Jim stepped back from his dropped gun, and looked at Angela, who was still on the floor, a hand held to one side of her face where Klein had struck her. He said: "You were right about him, Angela."

"What's that?" Klein demanded.

"She described you," Jim said. "Funny thing, Holt. I've known what you were for a

171

long time or I thought I did, but it's never quite the same when it's somebody else a man is fixing to kill, somebody like Tim Ryan."

Klein puzzled over what Jim had said for a moment, perhaps wondering how his wife had described him. Then, shrugging, he motioned toward the front room. Jim moved past him. Klein stooped and picked up Jim's gun belt, and followed.

Sam Pruett was in the big room with Yank Beeman and Zane Wheeler. Pruett grinned when he saw Klein with the gun in his hand. He said: "You'd better stay away from married women, hadn't you, Sheriff?"

Jim could not be sure how Yank Beeman and Zane Wheeler stood, although it was reasonable to assume that they were with Pruett, since they were the ones who had delivered the calves to Howdy Gale. The only weapon Jim had was the bill of sale, and it was possible that he could use it to drive a wedge between Klein and the others. He wasn't sure it would save his life, for, even if he got Klein off his neck, he could expect no mercy from Pruett, but at the moment he could think of nothing better.

"Looks like it, Sam," Jim said. "And along that same line, you'd better stay away from stolen calves."

Jim's words wiped the grin from Pruett's face. Ordinarily he masked his real feelings behind a veneer of laughter and amiable talk, but there was no veneer now. He took a step toward Jim, eyes switching to Klein and back to Jim, then he said, tight-lipped: "A man had better steal calves than wives, Bruce."

"That might be," Jim answered. "You're down on both charges. I've got a hunch Holt don't know about his wife or the calves."

Klein had come into the room. "Sam ain't got my wife, Bruce. He just wants her. I savvy that, but I don't savvy the calf talk."

Jim moved to the fireplace and turned so that he could watch all four men. Beeman had pulled his gun and was holding it on Jim. He said: "I'll take care of him, Holt."

"Why, now," Klein said, "I ain't in no real hurry. Let's hear some more about calves, Bruce."

"It's short and sweet. Beeman and Wheeler slaughtered your cows and delivered the calves to Howdy Gale."

"You got the deadwood on this hairpin, Holt," Pruett said. "Let Yank have him."

"I kind of like to hear him talk," Klein said. "Got any proof that you're talking straight, Sheriff?"

173

"You bet I have. And I'm wondering about Red Landers. Where is he?"

"Pulled out. Why?"

"About a week ago, didn't he? See him go?"

"What the hell we waiting for, Holt?" Pruett asked irritably. "This is what you've been wanting for a year and now you stand there listening to his guff. Well, you can listen, but damned if I am."

"Getting a little boogered, ain't you, Sam?" Jim said. "You've pulled the wool over Holt's eyes, and you sure hate to see me lift it off, don't you?"

Klein looked at Pruett, then at Wheeler and Beeman, and brought his gaze back to Jim. "What about Landers?"

"He's dead. Him and a couple other *hombres* I didn't know. They tried to kill old Chinook, figuring the mesa bunch would lay it onto you and come after you, but the scheme backfired. Landers talked to me before he died. Said Sam was offering a thousand dollars to the man who got me and Chinook. They had us holed up in the barn, but when they tried to root us out, they got some hot lead."

Pruett was walking toward Jim, his hands fisted. "You're lying, Bruce. Landers took his time and rode out."

"Then you paid a ghost, Sam. I was with him when he died." Jim pulled the bill of sale from his pocket. "Take a look at this, Holt. You know Sam's writing well enough, I reckon."

Pruett jumped at Jim, both fists swinging. Jim expected it, knowing the man would not let him go. He dropped the paper, ducked, and, coming up under the man's guard, knocked him flat on the floor with a smashing right.

"Damn it, Holt, you've got a gun!" Jim shouted, his eyes on Pruett. "Keep your rustler on the floor while you take a look at that bill of sale. I wasn't sure you were losing cattle till Howdy Gale gave this to me, but you were losing 'em, all right, and there's your man."

But Klein said nothing. Pruett rolled over and came up to his hands and knees. He looked at Klein, then got to his feet, smiling the way he did to cover his feelings. Jim did not understand it. He expected Klein to turn his gun, and, if he didn't, he thought that Pruett would bring the fight to him, but now he saw that the K Cross foreman had no desire to fight.

It was not until Jim stooped and picked up the bill of sale that he saw what had happened. He turned to Klein, holding the paper out, then he dropped his hand to his side. Angela had come through the hall door behind him and she had rammed a gun against Klein's back.

"All right, Holt," Angela said tonelessly. "Take a look at the bill of sale. Might do you good."

Angela was holding a handkerchief to her cheek with her left hand. There would be a bruise under the handkerchief where Klein had struck her, but there were no tears in her eyes. There was anger and rage and humiliation. If Jim read her right, she would kill Klein if he made a wrong move, and, judging by the taut expression on Klein's face, he had the same idea.

"You missed a chance, Holt," Jim said. "Looks like we ain't gonna get another one."

"That's right," Angela said. "I'm sorry, Jim."

Pruett rubbed his jaw where Jim had hit him, the fixed smile still on his lips. He said: "This ain't the way we planned it, Angela. What's the matter with you?"

"Nothing. Holt hit me once too often. I told him the last time I wouldn't take it from him again."

"And I told you the next time you shined up to another man . . . ," Klein began.

Angela rammed the gun harder against his back. "Don't say it, Holt."

But Klein was like a mountain that was suddenly flattened to the level of the surrounding plain. His great shoulders were hunched forward; his eyes were swinging wildly around the room for Beeman and Wheeler, who were holding their guns on Jim, and Pruett, who was still rubbing his jaw. It was evident that the insolence that had been so much a part of him had been thoroughly whipped out of him.

"Everything I've done has been for you, Angela," Klein said. "I've built an empire and I aimed to go on building. When I married you, I was satisfied with what I had, but you. . . ."

"Oh, shut up," Angela said. "Sure I wanted you to be big, and what did it get me? I wanted to go to Denver, but, no, you wouldn't stand for it . . . I suppose you think that knocking me down like I was a man working for you is part of your empire building."

"Why should I let you go to Denver?" Klein bellowed. "You'd. . . ."

She pulled the gun back and hit him across the side of the head, a hard and vicious blow that brought him to his knees. He dropped his gun. She said: "Sometimes

177

the truth sounds pretty ugly, Holt, and you're not telling all of it. All right, Sam. You and Holt had better take a ride. Put his gun in his holster. Make it look like some of the mesa bunch had dry-gulched him."

"I've got a better idea. I'll take the tin star along and we'll fix it so it'll look like they got each other."

"No," Angela said. "The sheriff stays here."

Klein got back to his feet, reeling a little as if he were dizzy from the blow. He licked his thin lips, a gray beaten look crawling into his face. He said in a begging voice: "You can't do this, Sam. I knew how you felt about Angela, but I trusted you. You were the best ramrod I ever had."

"Sure I was," Pruett jeered, "but trusting me was your mistake. And you made another mistake when you said I didn't have your wife. You said I just wanted her. It's been a little more than that, my friend."

But Klein, with his luck run out, was no part of a man. There were twenty men in the high country who would follow his orders, but he had no way to reach them, and he saw that there would be no help. So Klein begged, crying out in a high, trembling voice, "You can't kill me like this, Sam.

178

Why, I've treated you like a son. If it's Angela. . . ."

"Shut up," Pruett said, picking up Holt's gun. "Funny how a man shows his caliber when the shoe's on the other foot." He turned to Jim. "I'll take that bill of sale."

Jim handed it to him, asking: "How come you signed that?"

"Howdy Gale wouldn't do business any other way. I wanted to get them into a tussle with Holt. Figured it was the easiest way to get rid of him. That's why we slaughtered the cows so you could see 'em. We had to kill Gray because he knew who done it."

"Dobe?"

"We didn't aim to do that. I wasn't there and one of the boys got spooked when Dobe poked his nose into things. He should have headed for town as soon as he saw the cows."

Pruett stuffed the bill of sale into his pocket and moved toward the door. Wheeler motioned to Klein. "Git along, boss. You heard the lady say we was taking a ride."

Klein moved to the door and went out into the golden sunshine, still lurching like a drunken man. Wheeler followed, but Pruett lingered in the doorway, questioning eyes on Angela.

"I don't get this about the sheriff," Pruett said. "What good will it do to keep him alive?"

"He won't do us any good dead," Angela snapped. "We can bargain with a live man. I don't aim to burn all our bridges till we know how we stand."

Pruett was not convinced, but apparently he sensed that this was no time to argue with her. He said slowly: "You're not dealing with Holt Klein now. If you've got any notion of double-crossing me. . . ."

"I still need you, Sam," she broke in, "and don't forget you need me. If there's any double-crossing, it'll come later, and I don't trust you entirely, either."

Pruett laughed softly. "Why now, honey, you've got no reason to say that." He nodded to Beeman. "Take the star-toter to the cellar and be damned sure you bolt the door. I'll be back before long."

Pruett went out then. Beeman said: "Move along, Bruce. The cellar stairs go down from the kitchen."

Jim hesitated, his eyes searching Angela's pale face. She turned away as if unable to meet his gaze, and he wondered if he would ever really understand the woman. Angela had gained a few hours of life for him, but in the end she could not hold out against

Pruett, who understood their situation better than Angela did.

"I ought to say thanks," Jim said.

Angela had walked to a window and stood staring into the yard. Without turning, she said: "No need to thank me, Jim. I've got my own future to think about. We've done a lot of scheming, but none of it has worked. Go on while I think. Sam and I can't afford a mistake now."

"If you have a future," Jim said, "it won't be with Pruett. How can you have any future with a man you don't really trust?"

She ignored his question. Beeman said irritably: "You going, Sheriff, or do I drag you down by the ears?"

Jim went then, along the hall and across the kitchen and down the stairs into the dank, cool cellar. The heavy door closed and he heard Beeman throw the bolt. He scratched a match, its tiny flame showing him rows of hams and sides of bacon hanging from the ceiling, barrels of flour and sugar and shelves of canned food. Then the match flame died.

He sat down on a box, knowing he should feel like a condemned man, but for some reason he did not. Angela would save his life if she could. He rolled a smoke and lighted it, shaking his head as he wondered how big a fool a man could be. If Angela was his only hope, it was a slim one at best.

Now, thinking about it realistically, the knowledge that he was a condemned man filled his mind. Only a miracle could save him, and at this time he could not see a miracle taking shape. But he was convinced of one thing. Expecting a miracle to save him was fully as sensible as trusting Angela Klein.

Chapter Ten

The prospect of death within the next few hours distorts a man's sense of time. Jim smoked one cigarette after another, glancing at his watch each time he fired a match, and finding that the minute hand moved with exasperating slowness. He tried to think how long Pruett was likely to be gone and what would happen when he got back, then he attempted to put it out of his mind and pin his thoughts on Linda, but invariably his mind swung back to his immediate danger, and a feeling of futility took hold of him.

It must have been more than an hour from the time Beeman had locked the cellar door that it opened and Angela came in, a lamp in one hand, her gun in the other.

"You know I can't let you go," Angela said, "so don't make me hurt you. I came down to talk. Beeman isn't very good company."

She placed the lamp on an upended box and, finding another, sat down upon it, her slim legs pressed tightly against each other, the gun in her lap. She was not attractive now; her face was pale and haggard, and her blonde hair was stringy and loosely pinned. For a moment her eyes, filled with deep misery, were fixed on him, then she dug a tobacco sack and a package of cigarette papers out of a side pocket and tossed them to him.

"I knew you'd just sit here and smoke," she said, "and that you'd go crazy if your tobacco gave out, so I brought you some."

It was thoughtful of her, and it woke a faint stirring of hope in him. He said — "Thanks." — and lifting his sack of Durham from his shirt pocket, held it up. "Had about one smoke left. I was wondering what I'd do when it was gone."

She smiled briefly as if her thoughts were far away, and for a moment he played with the possibility of reaching her before she could pick up her gun and use it. Then he dismissed it from his mind. It was better to wait and see just what had brought her here.

She must have read his thoughts, for she said: "Beeman's got a bottle, so he's enjoying himself, but he can hold his liquor. He'd kill you if you got past me."

"And he'd enjoy himself some more doing it."

"He'd like it, all right. So would Sam." She spread her hands as if she had come to the point where she could not think coherently. "I don't know what to do, Jim. I don't have any regrets about Holt, but I don't want them to kill you."

"I was wondering about that," Jim said.

"You shouldn't have wondered," she said sharply. "You should have known. It wasn't my idea that you come here today."

"You invited me. Remember?"

"But not today. Anyhow, I didn't know Holt would ride in when he did. And you had the bill of sale, so we had to do something. You don't blame me, do you?"

"No," he lied. "I don't blame you."

She kept on looking at him, the misery in her growing. This was a different Angela from the one he had seen before, the scheming and the pretense gone from her, and he sensed that for the first time in her life she was being honest with herself.

"You know how I grew up, Jim," she said, as if she were pleading with him to understand how she felt. "On a little old desert ranch that didn't have anything but a hard-scrabble range. No decent clothes. Not even enough to eat half the time, unless Dad was lucky enough to steal a steer. He never stole from our neighbors east of the creek. They weren't any better off than we were. He'd get one of yours or Tim Ryan's or somebody else's from your side of the creek."

Jim nodded, knowing it had happened occasionally. It probably still went on, although he had never thought K Cross's loss was enough to hurt Klein. Angela's folks were dead, but someone else was living in her old home, and there were others, out there on the dry and hostile desert, trying to get along where no one should have settled in the first place. He rolled another cigarette, and waited, wondering what she was getting at.

"We lived like animals," she went on. "Just thinking about ourselves and never sure where the next meal was coming from. What was wrong or right about a thing never entered our minds, so I sort of grew up with the notion that anything went, if you could pull it off. I had the same idea when I married Holt. Maybe I'm to blame for him starting out on what he calls empire building, but I didn't know how far he'd go. I want you to believe that, Jim."

Still he was silent, sensing again that she was trying to justify herself to him.

She leaned forward, hands clasped on her lap. "I don't know much about women, Jim. Holt fixed it so I never had any friends, but I know men. I know how they think and what they want . . . and mostly they're alike. If you promise them enough, they'll do what you want. Even George Waldron forgot he has a wife and four kids. Is there any decency anywhere, Jim?"

"If you look for it," he said.

She laughed bitterly. "I suppose I never looked for it." Then she shook her head. "No, that's wrong. I *have* looked for it. My world hasn't held any decency. I don't think I'm much different from other women. I want pretty things and a good time and money. When I got married I wanted children, but I can't have any. Doc Foster can tell you that. Maybe it's a good thing. Wouldn't Holt have had a devil for a son?"

"I reckon he would," Jim agreed.

Still her eyes were pinned to his face as if he had hypnotized her. She asked, her voice low: "You think I'm a bitch, don't you, Jim?"

"I ain't setting myself up to judge you," he said. "Won't make no difference, anyhow. If you don't get me out of here, I'm a dead man and you know it."

She made a quick motion as if to thrust his words aside. "I was thinking of you and me, and how you are different from the men I've known. I was thinking of you and Linda up there on Banjo Mesa. She took care of you and you lived in her home. I keep wondering what happened between you, and

187

you're probably telling yourself that she's good and I'm bad, and yet you say you aren't setting yourself up to judge me."

"You're Holt Klein's wife. That means something to me, even if it don't to Pruett and Waldron."

"All right. I made a mistake marrying him. You saw today how he treated me. It wasn't the first time he'd hit me, but I couldn't run away from him. You know that. What could I do, wanting to be loved . . . and having him for a husband? It was natural for me to turn to some other man. You can see that, Jim."

"All right. It was natural."

"But when I came to you. . . ."

"You had a string to it. You wanted me to smoke Holt down. Then you'd have been finished with me. All you wanted was to get Holt out of the way, and, if I'd done the job, the blame wouldn't have come back on you."

"You make me look pretty bad, Jim."

"It's true, ain't it?"

She shook her head. "No. I knew you were different, Jim. I knew it from what I'd heard about you a long time before I went to your place. If you weren't honest, you'd have made a deal with Holt like the other sheriffs did."

"I ain't like the other sheriffs San Marcos County has had," he said, "if that's what you mean."

"I meant more than that. You're in love with Linda, aren't you? You aim to marry her, don't you?"

"If I live."

She rose, her mouth a taut red line across her face. "I'll promise you one thing, Jim. You'll never marry her. And I'll say something else. You're the damnedest fool there is."

"You are a bitch," he said hoarsely. "You're the damnedest bitch I ever ran into. All you want is to get a man down on his knees to you. Maybe Holt had reason to bat you around."

She shook her head. "He never guessed. He was too sure of himself. He never even considered the possibility that any other man would have enough courage to touch his wife."

"Holt gets smoked down. So do I. K Cross goes to you, and you fix it so there ain't no law in San Marcos County except what Dobe Jackson gives it. That right?"

"That's the size of it," she answered. "Sam's got a bunch holed up in the hills above Gray's Crossing. Holt never knew they were there. Landers, Beeman, and

Wheeler were Sam's boys. They rode with the rest of his bunch the night they went after Chinook."

"What good did that do 'em?"

"None, but it would have, if you hadn't been up there. We've got big ideas, me and George Waldron. I'll marry him after he gets his divorce, and then I'll be a banker's wife. That's about as good as any woman can do. . . . We thought that if Chinook was killed, you and the mesa bunch would think Holt did it and you'd come after him. That left me in the clear. You see, George is afraid of public opinion. He'd never marry me if folks thought I had anything to do with Holt's death."

"What will people think about him divorcing his wife to marry you?"

"We won't be in any hurry. Besides, his wife will divorce him. She's already taken the kids and left the country."

"What are you going to do about Pruett?"

She shrugged. "He'll take his tough hands and get out of the country with a herd of K Cross cattle. That's his pay, and it'll be worthwhile."

"He won't leave without you."

"He'll have to. I told you George and me have big ideas. I don't aim to marry a rustler."

"What's this big idea of yours?"

She moved back to the door, her gun held at her side. She stared at Jim suspiciously as if wondering why he was asking questions. Then she shrugged as if it didn't make any difference. A dead man would not talk.

"A dam on the Wild Horse River," she said. "George and Delaney will put up the money and I'll put up the land. We'll sell to settlers, and George will use the bank to loan money to them. We'll be respectable and I won't be living like I do now, with everybody hating me because they hate Holt."

Respectable! That, Jim thought, was the reason for all the scheming and lying and double-crossing she had done. Living here as she had, she had come to value respectability above everything else.

It was funny, if a man could see any humor in such a thing. Waldron and Angela had had the same notion he'd had, but in quite a different way. Waldron would use the bank to loan money, then foreclose and sell the land again. In the end, Angela would find herself hated as George Waldron's wife just as she was hated now.

"I have one thing to thank you for, Jim," Angela went on. "We need the law. It hasn't meant anything in the past, but it does now, because you've made it mean something.

191

For a year you've stood against Holt, so he's had to walk easy. A new sheriff, even a kid like Dobe, will have an easier time because of what you've done."

"While ago, I thought you'd come down here to save my hide," Jim said, "but I guess I was wrong."

"A woman has a right to change her mind," she said somberly. "You didn't want me. I was another man's wife."

"Hell, you never meant anything you ever said to me. You've lied so much you don't know when you're telling the truth."

She was silent, her face grave and showing no resentment. Finally she said: "You're wrong, Jim. Maybe I've been two different women, both of them wanting different things. You see, one side of me wanted your kind of life, and I had a wild idea you'd help me live it. But I'll have to settle for the other. Being a banker's wife won't be so bad. Before we're done, a thousand people will live here in the valley, and in the end everything I've done will be for the good of everybody."

She was trying again to justify herself, and it still made no sense to him. He would never understand this woman, and he doubted that she understood herself. She had been unhappy, and with reason, but the things she was doing would not bring her happiness.

Angela turned toward the door, and in that instant Jim heard a faint sound on the stairs. He was not sure whether it was real, or the product of an imagination fed by his taut nerves. He called — "Angela!" — knowing that if someone was on the stairs who was his friend, Angela's gun might ruin the slim chance of escape that he had.

She swung back, a smile of anticipation breaking across her face. "So you're going to beg," she said. "You're too late, Jim."

"No. I was wondering how long Waldron's had this big idea of his."

Disappointment wiped the smile from her face. "A little less than a year. Why?"

"What do you know about this Smoke Malone?" he asked, ignoring her question. "I thought maybe he was in on the game."

"Never heard of him," she said.

"I don't see no sense in this calf stealing of Sam's," he said, desperately trying to hold her and hoping someone was on the stairs.

"He had to have some quick cash to pay for men," she said. "That was the only way he could get it."

"Why didn't Waldron give him . . . ?"

It was then that Linda slipped into the room, a Winchester in her hands. Angela must have seen the swift run of relief that lighted his face. She whirled, but she was too late. Using the butt of the rifle, Linda struck her on the back of the head and knocked her down.

"I ought to have shot her," Linda said. "I've been out there a long time listening to her. Hanging's too good for a she-devil like that."

Jim was shocked by what Linda had done, but he said nothing as he stooped and picked up Angela's revolver. The woman was unconscious. He felt of her wrist. The pulse was strong and regular. When he rose, he looked at Linda, and the girl must have sensed his feelings.

"I had to, Jim," Linda said. "Beeman's in the front room. I sneaked through the back door without him seeing me, but we probably won't get out that easy. If I'd shot her, he'd have had us trapped down here."

Jim nodded, knowing that what she said was true. They left the cellar, Jim bolting the door, and climbed the stairs. Angela's gun was too small to be effective except at close range. He searched his mind for the best course of action, and could think of nothing that held any real promise. But he was certain of one thing. He could not have Beeman in the house, alive and free, and he didn't want to be handicapped with a prisoner. His first responsibility was to get Linda away from here.

He reached the kitchen a stride ahead of Linda, and saw Beeman coming down the hall from the front room. The man must have heard something that alarmed him, or perhaps he was only looking for Angela. Jim never found out, for Beeman saw him then; he let out a squall and dug for his gun.

Jim fired, the small revolver barking with brittle sharpness. Beeman stopped as he swept gun from leather and pulled trigger, a wild shot that slapped into the wall behind Jim. Beeman had been hit, and the pressure of his fear had made him hurry his shot. Linda's Winchester cracked and Beeman took a step forward, his gun slanting downward as it roared again. Jim's second shot got him through the head just above the nose; it brought him down in a loose-limbed fall and left him motionless on the floor.

"We've got to get out!" Linda cried. "Your horse is still in front of the house. Mine's in the back."

Linda was through the back door then, running in lithe strides toward her horse, and Jim remembered that Sam Pruett would be along soon. He raced out of the house and reached the end of the porch as

Linda stepped into the saddle.

No one was in sight. He ran around the house to his roan, grabbed the reins, and swung into the saddle as Linda thundered across the yard to him, screaming: "We've got to run for it, Jim!"

He whirled his gelding in beside Linda's horse, catching a glimpse of Pruett and two other men in the aspens above the buildings. Jim Bruce had never ducked out of a fight in his life, but, because of Linda, he had to duck now, and he thought with bitter self-condemnation that he should have taken time to find his gun, or at least pick up Beeman's. It was too late now.

Pruett yelled and, grabbing his Winchester, threw a shot that sang high over Jim's head. In that instant Jim had to make a decision. He and Linda could take the road to Harmony. If they could reach town, they would be safe, for Pruett would not follow them that far, but Pruett rode a fast horse and it was unlikely they would ever get to Harmony.

The other possibility was to head for Gray's Crossing. It was miles closer, and, once they had forded the river and were on the mesa, Pruett would turn back. With only two men, he would not want to tangle with Howdy Gale and his neighbors.

There was no time to think about it. It was a split-second decision that, once made, was irrevocable. Three things decided him: the distance, Pruett's fast horse, and Howdy Gale's promise to help when he was needed.

"We'll try for the Crossing!" Jim yelled, and, turning his horse off the road, headed south.

Chapter Eleven

Pruett's yell had been slapped out of him by surprise; he had pulled his rifle and fired without thought. But surprise was only momentary, and he was not a man to waste lead at this distance. Now he settled down to the chase, his two men beside him. Looking back, Jim saw that it was going to be touch and go. His roan would make a race out of it, but he was doubtful about Linda's mount.

For a mile the gap between them remained the same, then Pruett began moving ahead of the men with him and Linda's horse slowed down.

Jim, riding low in the saddle, glanced back at Pruett, mentally measuring the distance ahead and trying to judge the rate of Pruett's gain, but he could still not be certain of the outcome. He was holding his roan down to match Linda's speed. They could make it, he thought, if Linda's horse kept his present pace, but it was his guess that the animal would continue to slow down until Pruett caught them or came close enough for accurate shooting. If Jim's judgment of Pruett was right, the man would kill both of them.

The aspens to their right fled by, their trunks making a white blur. The wind slapped at Jim and Linda, sucking at their nostrils until it was hard to breathe, and the sun, well down toward the Ramparts now, threw long, leaping shadows into the grass beside them. Again Jim glanced back. Pruett had narrowed the gap by ten yards or more, and now he was far ahead of the other two men.

"My horse is about done!" Linda cried. "Go on, Jim. You can make it!"

"No!" he yelled. "Keep going!"

They had covered half the distance to the Crossing now. Pruett fired, the bullet coming close to the side of Jim's head. At this rate, another mile would bring him close enough to knock Jim out of the saddle. Linda would be next.

Linda turned her head to look at Jim; he saw the set expression on her face, then she yanked her Winchester from the scabbard and, turning in the saddle, threw a shot at Pruett that sent his hat sailing. Pruett must have guessed then that Jim was not armed; he tried for Linda with his next shot. Jim saw the flick of her coat sleeve. He shouted: "Gimme the rifle!"

She didn't hear. She turned and fired

again, hitting Pruett's horse and bringing him down in a rolling fall that sent Pruett pinwheeling through the air to land on his back. Relief rushed through Jim. He thought: *We'll make it now.*

Pruett's horse was finished, but Pruett jumped to his feet, grabbing up his rifle and taking careful aim. Linda fired before he could pull trigger. He went down and lunged to the cover of a nest of boulders. His men reached him then and reined up.

Jim felt like shouting a derisive yell of triumph, but no sound came from his lips. In that instant, Linda's horse, staggering with fatigue, went down and threw the girl. Jim turned back, calling: "Get up with me!" Then he saw that she had been knocked cold by the fall.

It took precious seconds to swing down and pick her up, more seconds to get back into the saddle. She made a slack burden in his arms as he whirled his roan and dug in the steel. Firing broke out behind them and the air was filled with the snap of hungry lead.

It was not until he was fifty yards farther on that he thought of the girl's Winchester. It didn't make any difference. He could not have used it with Linda in his arms, and it would have meant more wasted time if he

200

had hunted for it, time that might have meant the difference between escape and death. His one thought now was to reach the river.

Howdy Gale might have someone at the Crossing, or at least not far away. The sound of firing would bring help. Pruett probably had the same thought, for, when Jim looked back, he saw that one of the men was on the ground and Pruett had taken his mount. The horse was slower than the one Pruett had lost, but Jim's roan was not as fast now with his double burden, and again the pursuers were closing the gap.

If anyone was up there on the mesa, he was not buying into the fight. Then Jim realized with stark clarity that he could not get to the top of the mesa hill. His roan was too far gone. Or even if he did, he would be slowed down to a snail's pace and Pruett could pick them off like pigeons on a barn roof.

He felt the girl stir in his arms. She tried to sit up, and he shouted: "Take it easy!" It struck him then. The river! Gray's boat! No one had ever run the gorge. Perhaps it could not be run, but it offered a chance for life, and death was certain if he forded the river and tried to reach the mesa.

Jim angled his horse downstream and

rode over the last rise and down the steep pitch to the river. The carcasses of the cows were still there, the stench an offense to his nostrils. Gray's boat was tied to a willow, just as the old man had always left it. Jim reached the edge of the water and, swinging down, carried Linda to the boat.

"Are you crazy, Jim?" the girl cried.

He didn't answer. There was no time to argue with her. Probably he was crazy. He had been for a long time. Crazy when he had clung to the hope that Angela would free him. Crazy when he had thought he'd heard someone on the stairs. Crazy even to think he could battle K Cross and bring justice to Wild Horse range.

He worked at the knot with frenzied fingers. Too tight. He couldn't untie it. He got out his knife and slashed the rope in two. He had been holding the boat with one hand, and now he jumped into it as Pruett topped the bank above him.

"Don't try it, you fool!" Pruett yelled.

That was crazy, too, Pruett saying that. Jim didn't look up. The boat was in the water, the walls of the gorge slipping past. He got the oars into the oar locks; he dipped them into the water as he heard the beat of gunfire above the roar of the river. A bullet slapped into the seat beside him, another whipped into the stern and sent splinters flying. He was using the oars then against the implacable pull of the torrent; he missed a rock that lifted its ugly head above the white froth, and he thought: *There's a million more ahead of us . . . and I can't miss 'em all.*

Linda was huddled behind him. She screamed: "Beach it, Jim! We're out of rifle range."

There was a narrow sandbar to his left. He pulled on the oars, angling the boat toward it. The river was a beast, a white-maned, ugly beast that was hungry for their lives. For a moment, he thought he had missed the bar. He yelled: "Jump!" He saw the girl leap out of the boat onto the wet sand; he had the bow against the bar and for a moment he held it there, muscles straining as he tried to force it high enough on the bar so that he could leap out and drag it up out of the clutching pull of the water.

Sweat burst through his skin, and the futility of trying to run the gorge reached into his mind. He had known the men who had tried. They had never been seen again.

He wanted to beach the boat, to pull it clear of the water and hold it; he wanted time to think and talk to Linda and decide whether they should run the gorge. He couldn't. In spite of all he could do, he was losing the boat. It slowly slid around and briefly held against a rock, and, over the thunder of the river, he heard Linda scream: "Jump, Jim! Get out!" She was holding the bow, her feet braced against a rock ledge at the shallow edge of the water. A few inches from the ledge, where she had braced her tall heels, the bank dropped straight down, and anyone falling into that boiling, devil water would be smashed to death at once.

He must have been insane through those seconds, seconds that seemed an eternity, an insanity that reached back into his boy-hood when he had stood beside the river below the gorge and promised himself that someday he'd run it if it was the last thing he did. If he lost the boat, he'd never run it.

"Jump, Jim! Jump!"

Linda kept screaming it, over and over. He obeyed then, dropping the oars and leaping toward her. The boat whipped out from under him; he hit the shallow water around the ledge, and it splashed up around him. For one sickening moment he thought he had failed; he couldn't seem to get the solid footing he needed, and he felt the shocking chill of the river that was born in the snow of the high Ramparts. Then Linda was yanking at him, and he fell forward onto the bar and crawled until he was belly-flat on the sand. He lay there, motionless, bone-weary.

Slowly he raised himself on his arms and looked downstream. The boat was a tiny rocking bit of flotsam. Even as he looked, he saw it sweep sideways against a rock.

He sat up, wiping a hand across his sweaty face, and he saw that Linda was crying. He reached for her and she came into his arms, her head against his soaked shirt. He held her that way for a long time, the last of the afternoon sunlight full upon them.

He pushed her away and looked at her. "We're alive," he said softly.

She clutched his arms, bruised knuckles red and blue. "I thought you weren't going to be, Jim. I thought you weren't."

He laughed shakily, reaching for tobacco and paper. He pulled the soggy sack and package of papers from his shirt pocket, looked at them in disgust, and threw them into the river.

"I wanted to save the boat," he said. "I thought we'd rest and go down the river. Wouldn't take long to get out of the gorge the way the water rolls through here."

"Doesn't take long to die, either."

She was right. The old challenge of the river was gone now. He was glad he was here, glad he was still alive. He looked at her, seeing the hunger that was in her face, and he knew she felt the same way he did. It was no time for them to die.

"You shouldn't have come after me."

"I had to," she said. "I was mad when you wouldn't take me. Hurt, too, I guess. Then I thought about it, and I could see how you felt, but I just couldn't let you do a crazy thing like that alone. Jim, sometimes I think you aren't very bright."

"I ain't. When I was little, my mother dropped me down a well to see if I'd bounce. I ain't been bright since."

"Oh, don't be a fool. I mean you take the craziest chances. I know you thought the bill of sale would convince Klein that we weren't stealing his cattle, and would turn him against Pruett, but I still say it was crazy to go in alone that way."

"It would have been crazier to have taken Howdy and the boys with me." He was silent for a moment, thinking it would have worked if it hadn't been for Angela. Then he said: "I still don't savvy how you happened to show up when you did."

"I followed you. Kept up in the aspens so you wouldn't see me. I watched the house, and, when Pruett and Wheeler left with Klein, I was pretty sure you were in trouble. Wheeler took Klein and headed into the hills. Pruett lit out for the Crossing."

"You must have waited a while after that."

She nodded. "I didn't know what to do. I couldn't tell whether you were alive, and I had to find out." She looked away. "Seemed like it didn't make any difference whether they killed me or not. I just wanted to know about you. I got into the kitchen without Beeman seeing me. Didn't expect anybody, I guess. Then I heard you and Angela talking, and I went down the stairs."

"I'm beholden. . . ."

"Don't say that," she broke in. "I owe you more than you owe me."

"Why, that's crazy. . . ."

"Jim, Jim, don't you understand? The way we've lived, like savages, fighting and hating outsiders and being afraid all the time." She shook her head. "No, you couldn't understand. I guess I just started to live when you came home with me that night." She clenched her fists, staring at the river. "I heard some of the talk between you and Angela. She's no good, Jim . . . she's just no good."

He reached out and took her hand; he was silent for a moment, wondering how much she had heard. Then he said: "I don't savvy how you knew Pruett was coming."

"I didn't. I got boogery, Jim. Just plain scared. We'd killed Beeman. Seemed like . . . all of a sudden . . . I couldn't stand it. Had to get out."

He nodded and rose, understanding how it had been with her. She had been frantic with worry from the moment he had left her that morning, and it had caught up with her. He understood something about Linda that he had not understood before. She had lived outwardly like a Gale, but underneath the tough exterior that masked her real feeling, she was hungry for the same things that a valley woman hungered for.

"Ain't got too much daylight," he said. "We've got to get out of here."

She said nothing, sitting motionlessly on the sand, her eyes on him. He walked the short length of the bar and came back to her, thinking of the possibilities. They couldn't get across the river and they couldn't swim upstream or walk along the edge to where the boat had been tied. Just one other chance. The cliff!

He stepped to the edge of the sand and looked up at the steep sandstone wall of the gorge. They were not far below the Crossing, but they had swung around a bend so that Pruett had lost sight of them. For a moment he considered the possibility that Sam Pruett might be waiting for them on the rim, then he discarded the thought. Pruett would be sure that they had drowned. It had long been a common belief that anyone entering the gorge had committed suicide. By now, Pruett would be halfway back to K Cross.

Linda sensed what Jim was thinking, and said in a low voice: "We can't do it, Jim. I'm scared of high places. I'll get partway up, and freeze. I just can't."

He walked to her and, taking her hands, brought her to her feet. He said: "When you've got to do something, you can do it. I've been scared plenty of times lately. You said I took the craziest chances. Reckon I have, but my luck's been good. We've got to believe it's still good. Not just my luck, Linda. Our luck."

She nodded, trying to smile. "All right, Jim."

He looked at the cliff again. It was not as high here as it was farther downstream. If they had gone another fifty yards, there would have been no chance for them. Now, studying the broken face of the wall, he thought there was. He could see ledges that were wide enough to support a person, and at this point both sides of the gorge stepped back, totally different from the precipitous walls farther down the river that made the gorge a mere slit on the face of the plateau. Too, there were clumps of brush and runty cedars, precariously rooted, but probably strong enough to furnish handholds.

"Want to go first?" he asked.

She shook her head. "No."

"I'll try not to start any rocks to rolling, but watch out for 'em anyhow. The main trick is to not put your weight on anything that ain't solid."

She nodded, tight-lipped, trying hard to control the fear that was in her. She said in a low tone: "Go ahead, Jim."

He hesitated, his eyes locked with hers. He had no illusions about their chances, but no good would come from waiting. He said — "Let's start." — and turned to the cliff.

He began climbing, slowly, reaching up and searching carefully with his right hand until he had secured a handhold that could be depended upon. He reached the first ledge twenty feet above the river before Linda started. He waited there, watching her until she was beside him, pressing against the rough weathered sandstone.

"It won't be so tough," he said. "You see?"

"I see," she whispered. "Go on, Jim."

He started up again, pulling himself

through narrow crevices and being careful not to start a rock rolling that would develop into a thundering avalanche. At times he worked downstream, then angled upstream, gripping a rough trunk of one of the cedars or a clump of brush. Occasionally the roots tore out of their rocky footing, and he had to feel again until he found something that would hold his weight.

Every upward step was a gamble with death. He had never been bothered by high places, and he found it hard to believe that such a fear was in Linda. When he stopped to rest or to reach down and give her a hand, he realized that she was afraid, the kind of fear that stiffened a person's muscles and tightened one's nerves until each breath was an effort, but still she kept on.

She did not look down. That fact encouraged him. If she fell, there would be no living for him, no reason to keep on living. They talked very little, and, when they reached a ledge that was long enough to hold both of them, he put an arm around her, holding her hard against him as he tried to encourage her.

It happened when they were almost within arm's reach of the top. He was on a short ledge that broke off sharply on both sides. She was directly below him, clinging to a clump of brush with her right hand and to footholds that were barely large enough to hold the toes of her boots. She reached up to him and he took her left hand, pulling her upward until she was on the ledge beside him. But when her full weight was on the ledge, half of it broke off and roared down the cliff in a thundering cloud of red dust.

If he had not held onto her hand, she would have gone with the ledge. For one awful moment, she swung into space. An involuntary scream came out of her, a shrill sound that shredded his nerves, then he pulled her back up the cliff until her feet were solidly placed beside his.

There had been the one instant when he had been almost paralyzed, wondering if the rest of the ledge would go and whether he was strong enough to hold her. Then it was all right, and she was crying hysterically, clinging to him, her face buried against his shoulder, and he kept saying over and over: "We're all right, Linda. We're all right."

Presently the hysteria passed and she stopped crying. She whispered: "I'm ashamed, Jim."

"No need to be. We're almost up. The rim's right here. See?"

"Go on, Jim."

He was afraid to leave her, but they

couldn't stay where they were. He went on, scrambling another ten feet up the cliff that slanted away from the gorge, and there he found a well-rooted cedar. He paused, calling: "Come on!"

The river lay far below her, waiting hungrily for her, but still she did not look down. She came on up the slant, rapidly now as if using the last of her strength. He clutched the cedar with his left hand and, reaching down with his right, gripped her outstretched hand and brought her up beside him.

From this point the side of the gorge sloped back gently. There was soil here, a thin covering over the sandstone, and they climbed in a desperate, strained run, panting and laboring until they reached the level plateau. Stopping, he turned to her. She closed her eyes, swayed a moment, and fainted. As he caught her, he heard rocks that had been kicked loose by their feet roll over the edge to bounce down the cliff into the river, and the racket of their going was lost in the roar of the water.

He carried her along the rim toward Gray's Crossing, feeling a tenderness that was new to him. These last minutes formed a hell in his memory that would never be completely forgotten, and he knew what it must have been for her. It had taken courage, raw, tough courage that would have been found in few men.

His roan gelding was still there, not far below the Crossing, and he trotted up at Jim's whistle. It was dusk now, the sun hidden beneath the Ramparts, and Jim was filled with a sense of urgency. He had to get to town and raise a posse if he could. If he failed, he would ask Howdy Gale for help, but whichever he did, Linda would be safe in his house. In spite of his need to be traveling, he waited until she regained consciousness.

He knelt beside her in the grass, holding her hands. She opened her eyes, and for a moment she stared at him as if trying to remember what had happened. Then it came back to her and her hands gripped him in a paroxysm of returning fear.

"We're alive, Jim," she whispered. "We *are* alive, aren't we, Jim?"

"Sure, we're alive." He laughed softly. "You didn't think we would be, did you?"

"There was a time when I knew we wouldn't be," she said. "I fell ten million feet that time."

"Think you can ride now?"

"Of course. I never fainted before in my life. . . . What will Howdy say?"

214

"He'll be proud of you."

"No, Jim. He'll never be proud of me again. When you leave the mesa, you cut all your ties. I cut mine this morning."

"It was time," he said. "No use thinking about the past. Tomorrow looks good to me."

"Tomorrow." She said it softly, almost as if the wonder of its promise was too much for her. "Yes, Jim, it looks good."

He took her up in front of him and they rode toward Harmony, his arm tightly about her slack body, and she lay like that, her eyes closed.

Chapter Twelve

It was fully dark when they reached Harmony. Even the thin star shine was blotted out by thick clouds that had drifted westward from the Ramparts, and thunder was an ominous rumble that beat irritatingly at Jim's taut nerves.

Perhaps it stemmed from his weariness, or from the weakness that comes after a close brush with death, but, whatever the cause, Jim found his jumbled thoughts turning back to his childhood, to his mother's strange fears about storms and darkness.

Now, with his thoughts running in a weird, almost incoherent stream, the notion struck him that he and Linda had died in the gorge. He reined up in front of the Chinaman's restaurant, shivering a little as he took a grip on himself.

He eased Linda down, and for a moment she stood looking at him, sensing that something was wrong. She asked: "What is it, Jim?"

He was surprised at her resilience, at the way an inner core of strength fed her body.

He swung down, his knees wanting to buckle under him, and it took a moment to gather his thoughts enough to answer: "I'm loco. Can't get that climb out of my head. Seems like we died back there."

She gripped his hand. "I know, Jim. We'll never be the same again, either one of us, but there's still a lot to be done."

"That's right. Well, there's nothing wrong with me that a steak a foot long covered with onions won't fix."

An hour later, he sat back and patted his stomach, a sense of drowsy well-being flowed through him. "Want to go to a hotel?" he asked Linda.

She seemed to freeze, her hands fisting on the counter in front of her. "No. I've never been to a hotel in my life. I wouldn't know what to do."

He nodded, understanding how she felt. "You can sleep in my house. There's a cot in my office I can use."

She smiled shyly and slid off the stool. "I'd like it that way, Jim."

He paid for their meals and they went back into the street. He said: "Might as well walk. I've had all the riding I want for a while."

She walked beside him at the edge of the dust strip, Jim leading the roan. It seemed to him that all he wanted was sleep, a solid week of it, and then another steak like the one he'd just eaten, and a quarter of one of the Chinaman's peach pies.

Linda said nothing until he had watered and fed his horse. Then, while he rubbed the roan down, she asked: "What are you going to do, Jim?"

"Sleep."

They walked across the yard to the back door of the house, lightning flickering above the Ramparts in crackling veins of fire, and the thunder seeming closer now. They went in, and Jim lighted a lamp on the kitchen table. He turned to look at her, remembering what she had said about cutting her ties and that Howdy would never be proud of her again.

"How will your brothers get along without you?" he asked.

"They'll get along," she said, tight-lipped. Her eyes met his, her tan face expressionless. "I'll never go back, and I'm not sorry. I'm glad you came along, Jim. If you hadn't, I suppose I'd have kept living just the way I was, but from now on I aim to live my life the way I used to dream I would."

He put his hands on her shoulders and brought her toward him. She held her body stiff, and he saw something in her face he did not understand.

"You'll live your life with me," he said. "I'm glad I came along, too."

She shook her head and pulled his hands down from her shoulders. "I was thinking all the way in, Jim. It won't do. Look at me . . . wearing men's clothes and riding and fighting like a border tough." She swung a hand out to an all-inclusive gesture toward the table and stove. "I wouldn't fit, Jim. You can see that. This is town. You belong here. I don't. I can't serve tea and biscuits to other women when they come calling on the sheriff's wife."

"This is town all right . . . and a hell of a town it is," he said angrily. "That's the craziest talk I ever heard. There ain't a woman in Harmony who knows how to serve tea and biscuits, or whatever it is they serve. Wouldn't make no difference anyhow."

He took her in his arms again and kissed her. She struggled for a moment, fighting her pride and her resolve, and then she gave in to him, returning his kiss with a deep passion that told him better than any words she could use how great was her hunger for him.

She drew back, her hands coming up to his face. She whispered: "I'm a fool, Jim, to think it would work, but it's what I want.

It's you I want more than anything else in the world."

"We'll get married tomorrow," he said.

"Tonight, Jim. I'm afraid to wait."

He took a long breath, knowing that nothing had changed since this morning when he had said he wouldn't marry her and make her a widow. The shadow of the next hours lay heavily upon him, but he could not tell her that. "I'll see if I can find the preacher," he said, and left the house.

The preacher was not in Harmony that night. There was only one preacher in San Marcos County, and he had left at sunup to preach a funeral in the desert, thirty miles away. He would not be back until the next afternoon.

Linda took one look at his face when he returned and nodded as if she had read his mind. "He wouldn't come, would he?"

"Gone," Jim said. "Won't be back until tomorrow."

She stood with her back to the stove, her dark eyes on him. She said: "It's a sign, Jim. We're not meant for each other."

"Don't be superstitious," he said irritably. "I thought this morning I'd lost you. I won't let it happen again."

He stood in the doorway that led into the living room, knowing he should go and not wanting to. She moved around the kitchen, touching his things, and, when she came to a piece of glassware that his mother had brought across the plains, she took it down from the cupboard and held it in the light.

"Cut glass," she said reverently. She put it back and came to him. "Jim, is it wrong to want to live like this and have nice things? You know, the things Howdy calls foofaraw?"

"Of course not."

"I keep thinking about the way I was raised, wanting things I never thought I'd have. Howdy won't change. Neither will the other boys, but the rest of the world will change, and the mesa won't be backwoods forever."

"No, and neither will the valley. You heard what Angela said about the valley, about the big idea she and Waldron had?"

She nodded. "I thought it was funny, them having the same crazy dream you had."

"It ain't crazy. The land's good, and there's enough water in the river to irrigate a valley twice this big. It's bound to come when a company that has enough money to build a dam gets interested in the valley."

She nodded absently, as if her mind was on something else.

"I guess I'd better go," he said.

She said nothing while he picked up the lamp and went into the bedroom. He took a Colt and gun belt from the bureau, checked the .45, and buckled the belt around him.

He returned to the kitchen and set the lamp on the table. "I don't look for no trouble tonight, but you'd better stay inside," he said.

"I'll be all right." She stood in front of the stove again, straight-backed, the weariness gone from her. Suddenly she came toward him. "Jim, stay with me tonight. I keep thinking about what you said, about having died in the cañon. It's crazy to talk that way, but it isn't crazy to think of what's ahead. This might be the only night we'll ever have together."

She said it simply, her voice leaving no doubt in his mind about her feeling for him. He could not help comparing her to Angela. She was straightforward and honest, and he had sensed a falseness in Angela from the moment he had found the woman in his cabin. He put out his arms toward her, wanting her and wanting her to know it. It was in that moment that powder flame bloomed in a bright rosette of light outside the kitchen window. The roar of the gun beat against his ear, the bullet splintering the door casing behind him.

For an instant he stood paralyzed, unable to grasp the meaning of this. Then he was filled with a wild fury as he thought that this moment might never come between him and Linda again. He dropped to the floor as the gun thundered a second time. Linda blew out the lamp and Jim came back to his feet and lunged toward the shattered window.

"Mighty poor shooting," Linda said contemptuously.

Jim pulled his gun and peered into the darkness, but he could see nothing that indicated the killer's presence.

Linda, beside him, asked: "Have you got another gun?"

"Stay out of it," he said sharply.

She laughed, the softness gone from her. "Ever hear of a Gale staying out of a fight?"

"You will this one. I've got enough to worry about without having you taking chips in the game."

"I'm in," she said quickly. "It'll be fun having a sheriff for a husband."

He said nothing, still peering into the darkness. He thought of Smoke Malone and Colonel Steele; he thought of the piece of obsidian that had been under old man Gray's head and the suspicion Doc Foster had had of the two men. This wouldn't have been Malone, or he'd be dead, but it might have been Steele.

"It wasn't Klein or Pruett," the girl said. "They wouldn't have missed."

"No, it wasn't either one of 'em," Jim agreed.

"Then who was it?"

"I don't know."

There was one good guess, a better guess than Colonel Steele. Waldron and Delaney wanted him out of the way, and this was likely the method they'd use. Whoever had fired the shots had fled by this time, and that was like them. They weren't fighters. Bushwhacking a man was just about their size.

"The whole town ought to be here by now," Linda said.

"Nobody but Dobe would have guts enough to look into a shooting," Jim said, "and I reckon he's still in bed."

"What are you going to do?"

"I guess I'll go to bed. You do the same. Lock the doors after I'm gone, and stay inside till sunup."

It was not what either of them wanted. He felt her hand on his arm, squeezing it, and he heard her say: "Won't it wait till morning, Jim?"

"Not after them shots."

He slipped through the door, shutting it behind him, and waited for a moment. The door had squealed as he had closed it, and he remembered he had planned to oil the hinges weeks ago. There was no sound from the sagebrush back of the house where the dry-gulcher had hidden. Waldron or Delaney? He could not guess which it had been. Waldron lived in the biggest house in town across the street and down half a block toward the business section. He'd start with Waldron.

He slipped off the back porch and moved around the house, keeping to the shadows. Reaching the street, he walked along it until he was opposite Waldron's place. There was a light in the banker's living room.

It took less than a minute for Jim to cross the street and swing around the patch of light that lay across the banker's front yard. He climbed over the railing at the end of the porch, cat-footed to the front door, and opened it. The long hall was dark except for a thin line of light beneath the door that opened into the living room. Still moving with extreme caution, he slid into the hall and, throwing the living room door open, went in.

Waldron was sitting on a leather couch, a book in his hands. He looked up, saw who it was, and laid the book down beside him. If he felt any shock at seeing Jim alive, he hid it behind an expressionless mask.

" 'Evening, Sheriff," Waldron said. "This is a surprise. I thought you were still on Banjo Mesa."

Jim had never liked George Waldron, a feeling that went back into his boyhood long before Waldron had called in the notes he had owed the bank. He had mentally appraised the man as being a little too soft for this country, but now he changed his mind. Waldron rose, anger growing in him as his dark eyes probed Jim.

Jim closed the hall door. "I want to see your gun, George."

"I don't have a gun."

"You're lying." Jim moved toward the banker, his face hard set. "I ain't here to play games, George. Let me see your gun."

"You're out of line, friend," Waldron said hotly. "In the first place, you break in here without an invitation, and, in the second place, you have no authority to ask for my gun."

"I ain't standing on authority tonight. Somebody just took a couple of shots at me."

Waldron's dark eyes seemed to narrow and sharpen. He moved back another step

226

as he said: "You're barking up the wrong tree, Sheriff. I don't have any reason to take a shot at you."

"You're lying again. I ain't forgetting what was said in Steele's office that afternoon, and I ain't forgetting what you and Delaney said to Doc Foster. Doc's my friend, George. That stunt was getting down pretty low."

"Get out," Waldron said. "Get out of here."

"Not till I see your gun. You giving it to me, or do I take it away from you and beat hell out of you while I'm doing it?"

A crafty expression had worked into the man's eyes. "No need for violence, Sheriff, but I'll tell you one thing. I'll remember this."

"It ain't all you're gonna remember." Jim walked toward the banker and held out his hand. "Let's have it."

Smiling as if he were anticipating his triumph, Waldron lifted a short-barreled Colt from his shoulder holster and handed it to Jim. "It hasn't been fired for a long time. Violence is your business, yours and Doc's, but it isn't mine."

Quickly Jim checked the gun and handed it back. Waldron had told the truth. If he had fired the shots, it had been with another gun. Jim said: "Was it Delaney?"

"Why do you ask that?"

"You two are sleeping in the same bed," Jim said bluntly. "Don't lie about that."

"I have no intention of lying to you." Waldron replaced his gun in the holster. "I have no idea whether it was Delaney or not."

Jim frowned, wondering whether he would get anything out of Waldron. He said: "I hear you intend to divorce your wife and give up your children, George. Think Angela's worth it?"

Waldron's face went slack, the craftiness gone from it. He threw a bitter curse at Jim, right hand grabbing for his gun in a wild, frantic motion, but he didn't fire. He had the gun clear of the holster when Jim hit him with a driving right fist that knocked him flat on his back, the gun clattering to the floor. Jim picked it up and slipped it into his pocket as Waldron crawled to the couch and leaned against it. He rubbed his chin, blinking owlishly at Jim.

"Start talking," Jim ordered. "I had quite a visit with Angela today. I know what you and Delaney and Angela are up to, but right now I want to know who was trying to drill me."

"I've got nothing to say," Waldron mumbled. "I think you broke my jaw, damn you."

"I wonder about Angela," Jim said softly. "She sent Klein out with Wheeler today, aiming for Wheeler to make her a widow. She'd have had me killed by now if I hadn't got away. Think you can ever trust her?"

Waldron came to his feet, right hand jerking a knife out from under his coat. Jim was caught flat-footed. He had never had a knife thrown at him before, and, like most men who used guns, he had always considered knife-throwers as the lowest form of humanity. Even when he glimpsed the shine of the naked steel, he found it hard to believe that Waldron would throw it. The knife came like a darting gleam of light, barely missing his throat and hitting the wall behind him.

Jim drove at Waldron then, the last bit of restraint gone from him. The banker let out a yell of fear and started to run. Jim grabbed him by the coattail and hauled him back, asking: "That a good sharp knife, George?" Waldron mouthed a fury-filled oath. Jim dragged him across the room to the knife. "I'll find out for myself how sharp that knife is. You know how, George?"

The toughness was gone from the banker now. His dark eyes protruded from his head; his lips quivered. Jim slammed him down on the floor and picked up the knife. He looked down at the trembling Waldron, balancing the knife by the tip between thumb and forefinger of his right hand.

"I used to be pretty good at sticking a knife into the ground when I was a kid," Jim said thoughtfully. "Haven't tried it for years. Wonder if I've lost the knack?"

Panic gripped the banker now, panic that makes a blubbering beggar out of what had been a man. He cried out in a breaking voice: "Don't do it, Bruce! What do you want?"

"Who took that shot at me?"

"Delaney. It was his turn tonight. We've been watching for you to get back."

"You'd do better with a kid like Dobe. That it?"

"Sure we would. He'll listen to reason, but you don't listen to anybody. You've got no right to judge me and Angela. We aim to put in an irrigation system. Any crime in that?"

"Murder's a crime."

"I've had no part in murdering anybody. I told Angela I'd marry her when she was rid of Klein and I had my divorce."

"What about Bill Gray. You kill him?"

"No. I stole the obsidian and gave it to

Angela. That's all I know about it."

For a long moment Jim stared at the banker's pale face, the knife handle rocking back and forth in his hand. Knowing all that Angela had done and planned to do, he had unconsciously tried to excuse her in his thinking. He could not excuse her now. Her beautiful face could no longer mask the evil that was in her.

"Get up." Jim tossed the knife across the room. "I'm throwing you into the jug."

Waldron got to his feet, still trembling. He breathed: "You have no charge to jail me on."

"Attempted murder will do."

"You think a jury would take your word against mine?"

"I'll give 'em a chance. Either way, you'll roost in the jug for a while."

Jim blew out the lamp and they left the house together, Jim a step behind Waldron, his gun in his hand. The next thing was to find Delaney, although locking him up with Waldron would not really settle anything. It was like cutting the branches from a poison tree. Digging out the roots was another matter.

Jim was certain of one thing. As long as Angela Klein was alive and owned K Cross, there would be no peace on Wild Horse range. Wherever she went, she could find men who would do her murder jobs for her, men who could be bought by what she had to offer.

Chapter Thirteen

Jim locked Waldron into a cell and returned to the street. There was no light in Delaney's store. The fat man lived in a small room in the back that was both kitchen and bedroom. When he wasn't sleeping or eating, he was working in the store.

Delaney did all of his own work, claiming he could not afford a man, but Jim had always thought it was a matter of stinginess rather than the inability to afford help. That was the key to Delaney's character. Angela had bought Waldron with a smile and a kiss; she had bought Delaney by promising him a fortune from the sale of irrigated land.

It took a few minutes to look into the Buckjack, to prowl around the store and make sure that Delaney was not there. Then Jim turned toward the hotel, thinking he could do nothing about Delaney until morning. There were a hundred places in town where a man could hide. If Jim did stumble onto the man, he'd probably get a slug before he had a chance to use his gun.

It was late, but Jim went on through the lobby to Molly Ryan's room in the rear of the building. She opened the door to his knock, smiled when she saw who it was, and stepped aside for him to come in.

"I heard some shooting a while ago," she said, "and I told myself you must be back. I never saw a man who attracted trouble like you do."

"I'm about done attracting it," he said as he stepped past her. "How's Dobe?"

"He's fine. Still weak enough to stay in bed, but he's eating like a horse and I think he likes to have me around." She closed the door and stood with her back against it. "What are we into, Jim?"

He shrugged, thinking there was no use to worry her with the story. "A mess. Where is Dobe?"

"The front room upstairs. He's asleep now."

"I'll wait till morning to see him. I've got some riding to do, and I was hoping he was able to go along."

She shook her head. "No chance of that, Jim. It'll be another week before he can sit a saddle."

He hesitated, searching for the right words. "Molly, you don't need to worry about Dobe and Linda. You see . . . me and Linda are getting married."

"You can't, Jim. That's the craziest thing

I ever heard. You and that wild woman! Why, there are plenty of women. . . ."

"She's not like you think," he broke in. "She's about the most wonderful woman in the world, I guess. I've been in love with her ever since I was up there on the mesa before election, but I never figured I had any chance."

"Well, it's your business," Molly said doubtfully. "You sound like you've got it bad."

He nodded. "I have. You'll like her as soon as you forget what people down here say about the mesa bunch. She's in my house now. We're getting hitched soon as I can get hold of the preacher. There never was anything between her and Dobe."

"I know that now. Dobe told me." Molly was silent a moment, thoughtful eyes on Jim. "Jim, Dobe's got a hunch. About Smoke Malone. Dobe thinks he's not just a gunman."

"Maybe Dobe knows what he is," Jim said irritably. "I've asked myself about that *hombre* till I'm loco, and I don't even have a good guess."

"Dobe didn't know, but he got the notion that a pair of guns was a perfect disguise for a man when he comes in to a country like this and wants folks to think he's something he isn't. And, Jim, I'm sure Malone is tied in with Colonel Steele. If you figure Steele out, you can do the same for Malone."

"How do you get that?"

"Nobody but Steele goes into Malone's room. He keeps the door locked. Makes his own bed. Sweeps out himself. I hand his linen through the door to him and he tosses the dirty linen out. You know that isn't natural for any man."

"I'll go see him." Jim turned to the door and paused there, a hand on the knob. "Molly, I'm beholden to you for taking care of Dobe. I'll put a bug in his ear about the way you feel. . . ."

"Don't you do anything of the kind," she said sharply. "Don't try playing cupid for me, Jim Bruce."

"Then I guess it's up to you to let him know. He ain't smart enough to figure out he's in love with you."

Jim went out, closing the door behind him. As he walked back to the lobby and climbed the stairs, he thought of what Molly had said about Malone and Steele, and he was remembering that Doc Foster had much the same idea about them. Malone's room was in the back, overlooking the alley. A single bracket lamp at the head of the stairs threw out a murky light, the ragged fringe of it reaching the door of Malone's room.

Jim moved along the hall, noting the thin light of lamplight that showed under the door. He paused, listening. Malone was talking to someone, his voice low and indistinct. *Steele,* Jim thought, *if Molly had been right about no one else going into Malone's room.* Jim knocked and Malone stopped talking. Jim knocked again, louder this time.

"Who is it?" Malone called irritably.

"Jim Bruce."

A long moment of silence followed before Malone asked, his voice still holding a note of irritation: "What do you want?"

"I've got to talk to you."

"In the morning. I'm busy."

"This is important. A lot of things have happened since I left town."

There was another moment of silence. Then Malone said, his voice friendlier now: "Look, Sheriff, I know trouble's been piling up on this range for a long time, and I hear you had some more on the mesa, but it don't concern me."

"I think it does."

"Oh, hell," Malone snapped, "go to bed. It's late. I've got to sleep whether you do or not."

There was nothing more that Jim could

do unless he wanted to batter the door down. Still, he stood there, thinking about Wild Horse range. If Klein was dead, and he probably was hours ago, the valley belonged to Angela.

Grazing land was never particularly valuable. On the other hand, irrigated land that could be sold in small tracts was a treasure worth fighting for. Angela knew that. So did Waldron and Delaney. A dream that had been nothing but a vague hope in Jim's mind had become the cause of more crime within the last few days than Holt Klein had been responsible for through the past year. That much was clear, but Malone's and Steele's part in the business was as big a mystery as ever.

Jim started back along the hall, anger stirring in him at Malone's hostility. The least the man could do was talk, unless he was into the whole business as deeply as Waldron and Delaney were. Jim turned back, struck by the thought that sooner or later Steele would have to leave Malone's room, and that would be Jim's chance to go in. Again he was guessing, but it seemed reasonable to think that the gunman had something in his room he didn't want Jim to see.

The door across the hall was ajar. Jim cat-footed to it and slid into the room. For a moment the door was partly open, the thin light from the lamp down the hall touching his face. When he closed the door, the room was black dark. He stood motionless, hand on the knob, listening for movement from Malone's room.

Jim thought with some sourness that he might have a long wait, and he should have been in bed hours ago. He was dead tired. The constant strain of these hours had caught up with him again. Even his whip-muscled body, hardened by a lifetime spent in the saddle, could stand only so much, and his had reached the end of its string.

He was close to falling asleep on his feet. It must have been the opiate of fatigue that dulled his usually alert senses. In any case, he was not aware of another man's presence in the dark room until he heard a floor board *squeak* under a heavy foot.

Acting by instinct, Jim dropped to the floor and rolled away from the door, grabbing gun from holster as he moved, a move that saved his life. A gun spoke ten feet from him. The slug slapped through the door, the explosion deafening as it hammered against the walls of the room.

A second later Jim's gun added to the racket. He fired three times, fast, holding his Colt low and tilting it up so that the bullets would catch the killer belt-high. He moved the barrel between his shots so that each slug was a foot or so to the left of the one before. Then he lunged to his right and waited, hammer back, holding his last two shells in reserve.

There was no sound for a moment after the throbbing gun echoes died except the labored breathing of the man who had tried to kill him. Then doors slammed. Bare feet pattered along the hall and someone kicked the door open. A shaft of light from a lamp held high in the hands of Al Hays, the hotel owner, washed into the room.

Pete Delaney was rocking like a great pine caught in a high gale, fat hands clutching his bullet-riddled belly, droopy-lipped mouth sagging open. Then he fell, full out, the room trembling as his heavy body hit the floor.

"What's going on?" Hays yelled. Then he recognized Jim. "Oh, it's you, Sheriff. Didn't know you were back." He saw that Delaney was dead, and his face hardened. "You played hell drilling Pete. I reckon they'll get your star now just like they've been talking."

Jim was on his feet, shoving cartridges into the cylinder. He asked: "You in the game with him, Al?"

Hays stepped back, worried. "I don't know what you're talking about."

Jim pushed past him into the hall. Dobe Jackson was there, clad only in a white nightshirt, his face pale and very thin. He said: "Didn't know you were in town, Jim. What happened?"

"Delaney was in the room. When I went in, he started shooting. It's the second time tonight he's tried to get me. Go back to bed, Dobe." He nodded at Hays. "Get your shutter and tote Delaney over to Doc's place."

Jim had been covertly watching Malone's door. It was open a crack. Apparently someone had been watching. Without warning, Jim threw a shoulder against the door in a driving lunge that slammed it open and knocked Malone flat on the floor. Jim slid into the room and closed the door, gun palmed. Malone sat up, swearing bitterly, and got to his feet, right hand falling to his Colt butt.

"Don't make me kill you, friend," Jim said.

Colonel Steele, standing at the window, cried out: "No, Malone!"

Slowly Malone's hand dropped to his side, his hard-bitten face holding an expression of unreasoning rage. "Damn you, Bruce! If you want trouble, you'll get it from me as sure as hell's hot."

"You ain't bright, Malone," Jim said evenly. "I don't want trouble. I want to talk. That's all."

"All right," Steele said. "Maybe it's time to talk. Sit down, Smoke. We've got to tell him, sooner or later."

Still muttering, Malone dropped onto a chair at the end of the bed, baleful eyes pinned on Jim's face. Jim had his first chance to glance around, and for a moment he was puzzled by what he saw. Books were stacked on the floor, more books than Jim had ever seen before in his life. A jumbled mass of papers were scattered on the bureau, all covered by neat, small figures. Some instruments were piled in the corner of the room beyond the bureau, surveyor's instruments and some more Jim didn't recognize. Suddenly the truth began to work into Jim's mind.

Steele stroked his goatee, smiling as he motioned toward the bed. "Sit down, Sheriff. From now on we're in the open, and I'll admit right now we should have let you in on it months ago."

"I ain't so sure about that," Malone snapped. "Bruce is a fair-to-middling sheriff to find in a country like this, but he's working against the current."

"Which maybe is our fault," Steele said. "I'll go along with a fair-to-middling sheriff if he's honest, and I think Bruce is."

Jim sat down on the bed. "Get at it."

"Frankly, Sheriff," Steele said, "we haven't been able to make up our minds about what should be done. I pretended to side with Delaney and Waldron that day in my office, mostly because I wanted Malone to finish his work before we took you into our confidence."

Jim had to fight his need for sleep as he sat there. He rolled a smoke, asking: "What kind of work?"

"What puzzles us were the uncertain elements that we found here," Steele went on, ignoring Jim's question. "You know as well as I do that this is a lawless country. Now I'll admit we've killed men when we had to, but only when circumstances forced us, as circumstances will eventually force you to kill Holt Klein."

"I won't have to. It's been taken care of." Jim read the titles of Malone's books, and now he brought his eyes to the man's face. "I've done some good guessing lately, but I missed this. So you're an engineer, packing two guns and looking tough just to throw us off the track."

"That's right," Malone agreed, "but don't make a mistake on one thing. I *am* tough."

"All right," Steele said testily. "Just forget you're tough, Smoke. I don't want the sheriff to think too badly of us." He nodded at Jim. "Look at it this way. Here is a potentially rich valley that might be worth a million dollars if we could buy it. If we were able to develop it, you'd profit, too, because we would put water on the land you've kept Klein from getting. The trouble is we've been stopped by the uncertain elements I mentioned. Take Klein. No good, Bruce. A bad one married to a woman who can look you in the eye and tell you she loves you while she sticks a knife in your back."

"How do you know that?"

"I think we know more about the folks who live here than anyone else in the valley." Steele smiled thinly. "We've ridden at night, we've spied on people, we've listened at keyholes. We're not proud of it, but we had to do it. I'm supposed to be a lawyer, Malone a transient gunhand. Nobody paid us much attention, but I made one mistake I've been regretting ever since. We like to work through the local bank, so I felt Waldron out. I told him enough to let him

244

guess why I was here." He spread his hands. "He fooled me, Bruce. I have no excuses. I just simply misjudged the man."

Jim toed his cigarette, fatigue beating at him. "Get on with it, Steele."

"Malone and I work for the Rocky Mountain Land and Water Company. We're interested in developing irrigation projects, but we are also interested in other resources. Timber. Mineral. Water power. This country is ideal except for one fact. Klein owns the valley and he won't sell."

"I told you he was dead."

"You see him die?"

"I saw Zane Wheeler take him out of the K Cross ranch house under his gun."

Steele shrugged. "I'll have to see the body, Bruce. I got the notion that Klein will be hard to kill. Anyhow, Malone came here to gather data on the possibilities of the valley. Amount of water flow. Site for the dam. That sort of thing. My job is to represent a feasible plan of operating. Malone has done his part, but I've failed on mine. I'll have to send in a negative report unless something happens very quickly."

"Ever talk to Angela?"

"No." Steele gave him his thin smile again. "I'm more afraid of her than all the men in the valley. She has been treated badly by Klein, so she has turned to George Waldron."

"I've got George in jail," Jim said.

Steele threw up his hands. "What kind of a charge have you against him?"

"Attempted murder."

The lawyer snorted derisively. "You might convict a man for horse stealing in this country, but you'll never get him for attempted murder."

Jim rose. "I'm going to bed. Hold that negative report for a few days, Steele." Jim walked to the door. Then he turned back, eyes on Steele. "Looks funny to me, you coming here with the same idea I had, and then Waldron and Delaney getting the same notion."

"It's not funny at all. You were responsible for all of it. I came here before you were elected, you'll remember. Just looking, pretending I wanted a place to retire. I heard some of your ideas and I got interested in this country because of it. I have no doubt that Waldron got the idea from me, and Angela got it from him."

"How come Delaney was hiding across the hall?"

"We have something he wanted." Malone pointed at the papers on the bureau. "My report is finished, Bruce. It's ready to go to the home office. I suppose Delaney listened outside and heard me tell Steele. If he could have stolen them, he'd have been saved a lot of money."

"Probably waiting for Smoke to leave the room," Steele said. "If he's been spying on us, he'd know that Smoke is gone almost every night."

"About that obsidian under Bill Gray's head. Waldron said he stole it and gave it to Angela."

"I'm guessing on that," Steele said, "but I have an idea Angela had schemed up a plan to get me and Smoke out of the way. She aimed to kill two birds with one stone. They wanted Gray off the river because he knew too much about the calf stealing, so they framed us for it."

"I wouldn't arrest you on that."

"I'm not so sure. Suppose Klein was found dead with a chunk of obsidian under his noggin. What would you have thought?"

"I'd have thought plenty," Jim admitted.

"It wasn't a good frame, but it would have done, I think," Steele said. "You knew I had the only obsidian in the country, and Smoke looked like a good candidate. Maybe it was the best Angela could think of. When you throw as much greed and hate into a pile as you have here . . . well, something's going to

247

happen, and Angela was gambling it would work the way she wanted it to."

Jim opened the door. "I'm all in. See you tomorrow."

"One more thing," Steele said. "I'll hold that report like you asked, but I have one suggestion. Don't push. Let this trouble ferment a little. Delaney's dead and you have Waldron in jail. Keep him there a few days."

Malone rose, his anger gone from him. "No hard feelings, Jim? I guess I should have listened to Steele, but I wasn't sure it was time to talk."

"No hard feelings," Jim said.

Malone smiled, the hardness leaving his face. "We all have our dreams, Sheriff. I think yours and ours aren't too far apart. Our company wants to make money, but we believe in a fair deal to the settlers. Our record proves that."

"So long," Jim said, and, leaving the room, went down the stairs and crossed the lobby.

For a time Jim stood in front of the hotel, staring up at the black sky that now and then was scorched by the shifting veins of lightning; he heard the rumble of thunder, but all of this touched only the fringe of his consciousness. He was thinking of what Steele and Malone had said.

It would take money to develop the valley, to make it a place where small ranchers could live and raise families. Money, a lot of it, to build a dam and a ditch system, to advertise the valley and bring settlers here. Jim had heard of the Rocky Mountain Land and Water Company. It had the money this job would take, and, as Malone had said, the company's record had been good.

Jim walked to the jail and, dropping down on the cot, pulled off his boots. Here it was right at his fingertips, the possibility of turning what people had called a crazy dream into reality. He lay staring at the black ceiling, trying to flog his tired mind into thinking of some means of opening the valley to settlement, but Klein had secured all of it except Pitchfork and the Ryan place.

It was a strange fate, Jim thought, that had given so much potential wealth to Holt Klein. Now it was Angela's. If she went ahead with Waldron, there would be neither happiness nor prosperity in the valley. Then he dropped off to sleep and lay like a dead man, not even aware of the storm that rolled down from the Ramparts.

Chapter Fourteen

It was not yet daylight when Linda shook Jim's shoulder, her words — "Wake up." — beating across vast space to a mind numbed by sleep. He sat up and pushed her away.

"Let me alone," Jim muttered, and, dropping back on the cot, turned over.

"You've got to get up, Jim."

"Let me alone," he said in a sleep-thick voice.

"I'm sorry, Jim, but you've got to get up. Angela Klein's here."

He sat up, jarred now into full consciousness. "Where?"

Jim pulled on his boots, fumbling for them in the dark. Then he scratched a match and lighted a lamp on his desk. Angela sat on one of his rawhide-bottom chairs, cold and wet, her blonde hair stringing down her face. She stared lankly at Jim as if she didn't see him. Looking at her, he thought he had never seen a person who appeared to feel as miserable as Angela did now. He wondered how he could have thought she was the best-looking woman in San Marcos County.

"What's the matter with her?" Jim asked.

"She just gathered her reaping and she doesn't like the crop she got," Linda said angrily. "Go ahead. Tell him."

Angela stirred. There was a dark bruise on one side of her face. Now she put a hand up to it, staring at Linda with a depth of hatred that Jim had never seen in her green eyes before. "Leave me alone. Go away. Leave me alone."

"I'll leave you alone when you talk," Linda hissed, "not before, and you'd better start, or what I gave you is just a beginning to what I'll do."

Angela slumped lower in the chair, putting a hand up as if to defend herself. "Get her out of here, Jim. She'll kill me."

Linda laughed scornfully. "I ought to." She swung to face Jim. "She's got quite a yarn to tell. Pruett told her you were drowned, so, when she got to town, she asked in the restaurant where Dobe was. The Chinaman said Dobe was still laid up, but you were here, so she came to the house looking for you."

"She said I was a wicked woman," Angela said in a low voice. "She called me a murderess. She said I had a lot of gall to come to you."

"I reckon you did," Jim said. "I wouldn't

251

be here if it wasn't for Linda."

"I wouldn't have let anybody hurt you, Jim," Angela whispered. "You know that."

"Oh, no, you wouldn't have let anybody hurt him!" Linda cried. "Send her back to Klein, Jim."

Angela began to cry, rocking back and forth in the chair.

Jim wheeled to face Linda. "Klein's alive?"

"I guess he is from what she says," Linda answered.

Angela put her hands to her face. "She hit me, Jim. Just like a man. Send her away. Don't let her hit me any more."

"I should have killed the lying devil!" Linda cried. "She said I belonged in a cave. She said I was out of place in your house. Said you'd do better to marry a Ute squaw." Linda turned away. "I guess it's true."

Jim put an arm around the girl and led her to the door. "It ain't true, and you're crazy for letting anything she says bother you. You go back to the house. I'll get her to talk."

Linda gave him a tired smile. "I'm crazy, all right, crazy for ever thinking it would work out. It's just that I wanted it to, Jim. I wanted it so much."

"You don't want it any more than I do,"

252

he said. "I thought you knew that."

She straightened, her pride taking hold of her again. "I do, Jim. It's the only thing I've got to hold to now." Turning, she walked out.

For a moment, Jim stood in the doorway, watching her until she had disappeared in the thin dawn light. Angela, he thought, had the mind of a devil. She had been surprised to find Linda in his house. Linda had made her talk and had struck her, and Angela had sensed the one great fear that was in Linda's mind. She had used her tongue brutally, just as Linda had used her fist.

Jim stepped into the room that held the cot and, picking up his gun belt, buckled it around him. He went back into the office and stood looking down at Angela, thinking he had never seen her brought as low as she was now. Her face was as expressionless as a perfect-featured dummy, but it was her eyes that held Jim's attention. She had a way of making them softly appealing to match the smiles that came so easily to her full-lipped mouth. Now they were like orbs of emerald, dulled by horror.

"She's gone," Jim said. "Now, tell me what happened."

It took a moment for Jim's words to penetrate her consciousness. She shivered, wet clothes clinging to her, and, when she raised her eyes to Jim, she seemed to be staring past him into vast space.

"You shouldn't blame me for what I've done," she whispered. "I only wanted what was rightfully mine. I've hated Holt so long that I went crazy. I'm crazy now." She raised a hand to her forehead. "I can't think. I'm not sure I'm alive. I keep seeing what they did to Sam."

"Who?"

"Holt and his men. He brought them down from the high country. Sam was in the house with me. Beeman and the two men Sam had with him were in the bunkhouse. Sam didn't have a chance for his gun. Somebody shot him. Then Holt beat him with his gun. He was bloody all down his face before he died. They killed Beeman and the others in the bunkhouse." She shuddered, hands fisting and opening on her lap. She started to get up and dropped back, then she began to cry, hysterical sobs that shook her slim body.

"How did Holt get away from Wheeler?" Jim asked.

She fought her hysteria for a moment before she answered. Then she said in a low tone: "Just luck, just plain fool luck. Wheeler should have shot him right after he left the house, but I guess he thought Holt was easier to handle alive than dead. Anyhow, he was taking him up Grizzly Creek when he ran into a couple of Holt's men coming downstream. They shot Wheeler, and Holt sent them back for the rest of the crew."

It seemed to Jim, staring down at the woman's bent shoulders, that this was a grim sort of justice. These were killings Holt Klein could not be blamed for. Anyone in the cattle country would feel the same way he had toward men who had robbed him and had been disloyal to K Cross. If Klein had not been so arrogantly proud, he would have seen what Pruett was doing a long time ago. But it was like Klein to trust his foreman, for the simple reason that he did not think anyone who worked for him would have the courage to double-cross him.

"How did you get away?" Jim asked.

"I don't know. I guess Holt was so busy with Sam he forgot about me. I ran out of the house and grabbed a horse. I got caught in the storm. I'm wet and cold, Jim. I'll get pneumonia."

"I'll take you to the hotel."

She rose and gripped the back of the chair to steady herself. "Before I left, I heard Holt

say he was coming after you. He's going to
burn the town and hang George Waldron."

Jim stood motionless, shocked by what
she had said, and thinking that it was another one of her lies. Then he knew he must
accept the possibility that she was telling the
truth. It was fantastic but possible. Klein
had always hated Harmony, just as he hated
the small restraints the county government
laid upon him.

There was something else, too. Klein was
probably out of his head. The close brush
with death, the indignities he had suffered,
the blow to his great pride that Angela had
given him — all were enough to make a man
like him go crazy. He had twenty salty men
who would be loyal to him, and he would
know that Jim could find less than a dozen
to defend the town. More than that, he
would blame Jim for much that had happened, and he knew that Jim would come
after him for the murder of Sam Pruett.

"Come on," Jim said. "You've got to get
those clothes off."

She went with him, swaying as if each step
was her last. Jim took her arm and she clung
to him frantically, whispering: "You're all I
have right now, Jim."

He didn't answer. They moved along the
wet boardwalk to the hotel, the sound of a

town waking up coming to them. The lightning and thunder had stopped, but the sky was still dark with clouds that hid the rising sun, and rain smell was strong in the air.

Listening, Jim could not hear the sound of fast traveling horses. He wondered if Klein would come, and if he did, when it would be? He knew there was no chance of out-guessing the man. But if Klein did come, and the conviction that he would grew in Jim, the K Cross man would have only one purpose, to slash and kill and burn.

Jim took Angela into the hotel and back to Molly Ryan's room. Molly opened the door to his knock, and, when she saw Angela, her eyes widened in surprise.

"What's happened, Jim?" Molly asked in a frightened voice.

"Plenty. Take care of Angela. No room in the jail for her, so I'm asking you to see she don't run off. Get her some dry clothes."

He wheeled and ran out of the hotel, a sense of urgency growing in him. He turned toward his office and went past it to the fire bell, grabbed the rope, and yanked on it again and again, peal after peal rolling out into the early morning silence.

It took only a few moments to get results. Half dressed men rushed into the street, throwing out questions, and, when they saw neither smoke nor flames, they ran toward the bell, shouting more questions at Jim.

Malone and Steele were there; Doc Foster, who had just returned from a trip across San Marcos Creek; Al Hays, the hotel owner — every man in town but Dobe Jackson, and Dobe threw up his window and looked out.

Jim paid no attention to their questions until they had gathered in a tight little knot in front of him. Then he told them briefly what had happened and what they could expect.

"On the face of it, we ain't got a chance," he told them. "You know what Holt Klein's like and you know the kind of men who ride for him. If you want to give up everything you own, get out of town. Move your women and kids. If you've got the guts it takes to stay and fight, go home and get your guns and ammunition and come back here."

"We'll all stay," Doc Foster said quietly. "This is the day Holt Klein dies. It should have come a long time ago. Them that have kids and wives can get 'em started toward the desert. Klein won't hurt them."

"I ain't staying!" Al Hays shouted. "I've got a wife and five girls. I'm looking out for 'em."

Others nodded and walked quickly away, hiding their fears behind the need of taking care of their families. Jim stared at their backs, rage blinding his vision. There was nothing he could do to make them stay. He could control his own fear, but he could not impart courage to other men. Only Doc Foster, Colonel Steele, and Smoke Malone remained.

"What are your plans?" Malone asked quietly.

"We'll fight," Jim said.

"You've got to have more of a plan than that."

"Doc, you and Steele hightail it over to the store and break out all the ammunition you can tote. We'll hole up in the hotel."

"The bank's a brick building," Malone said. "That's better."

"We can't move Dobe, can we, Doc?"

"He's weak yet. Better leave him in his room."

"What kind of sense is this?" Malone bawled, outraged. "Throwing our lives away because one man is too shot up to leave his room."

"He'll do his share of fighting from his window," Jim said. "If he starts running around, he'll cave."

"He's right," Steele said quietly.

"Give me a hand, Malone," Jim ordered. "I've got some Winchesters in my office. We'll tote 'em to the hotel."

"Wait." Malone grabbed his arm. "Hear that?"

Jim stood motionless, listening. It was a distant sound, but unmistakable, the beat of horses' hoofs, many of them, coming in on the road to K Cross.

"We've got five minutes," Jim said. "Maybe ten."

They hurried into the jail and came out with their arms full of rifles, their pockets jammed with shells, ignoring Waldron's pleas to be released.

As they ran toward the hotel, Malone said: "I'll get up on the stable roof. It'll be like shooting fish in a barrel."

"Go ahead."

They laid the Winchesters on the desk, the shells beside them. Malone picked up a rifle, balanced it in his hands, and sighted along the barrel. "This'll do." He jammed several boxes of shells into his pockets. "See you later, Jim. Good shooting."

Malone ran into the street. There was the commotion of Al Hays and his family leaving, his wife and girls dressed in night-gowns and robes, sleep-tangled hair streaming down their backs. As they hurried into the alley, Jim called: "Hold that buckboard up, Al, or I'll whittle you loose from your heart!" He grabbed a pair of Winchesters and some shells and turned toward the stairs.

Al Hays, sitting in the buckboard, cried out: "I ain't waiting. I've got to look after my. . . ."

"You wait, damn it!" Jim shouted.

"Our blood'll be on your head, Jim Bruce!" Hays screamed. "I'll haunt you and my wife will haunt you. . . ."

Jim didn't wait to hear the rest. The girls would haunt him, too, he supposed. He lunged up the stairs and along the hall to Dobe's room, threw the door open, and started to ask if Dobe had seen Molly. Then he held his question, for she stood at the window, Angela beside her.

"Al Hays is in the alley in his buckboard," Jim said. "Get down there, Molly. He'll get you out of town."

She whirled to face him, her mouth scornful. "You think I'll run like the rest of them?"

"You'll be safe. . . ."

"I can shoot, Jim, and I'm not afraid to stay and fight. I thought you knew me. . . ."

Angela came toward Jim, her face eager. "I'll go with Hays."

Dobe rose from where he had been sitting on the bed. "Don't let her, Jim."

Jim laid the rifles down, knowing that no matter what Angela had done, she would never hang. If Klein died today, Angela might be willing to make a deal for K Cross.

"You'll stay here, Angela," Jim said. "You'll be safer with us than you will on the desert." He nodded at Dobe. "Watch the street. I'll be downstairs with Doc and Colonel Steele. Malone's on the stable roof."

He swung back toward the door. Angela ran after him, gripping his arm. "I can't fight, Jim. Holt will kill me if he finds me here. Don't make me stay. . . ."

He looked down at her, the pale morning light upon her face. She was wearing one of Molly's dresses that did not fit her; she had not pinned up her hair and it fell in a yellow tangled mass down her back. A dirt smudge darkened one cheek. She had always been neat and completely at ease whether she was lying or telling the truth; now she was begging with a frantic fear in her green eyes that sickened a man. It was exactly as Linda had said. Angela was gathering her reaping and she didn't like the crop she had raised.

Her fingers dug into his arms. "I tell you he'll kill me. . . ."

"If he kills all of us, he'll kill you, I reckon," Jim said, "and maybe that'd be fair enough, considering what you've done, but if we live, we'll have a deal to offer you. You're staying because we can't afford to lose you."

He went out and along the hall to the back window. "All right, Al. You can dust!" he called.

Without a word, Al Hays cracked his whip and roared out of town toward the desert. Jim went down the back stairs. He could not hear the incoming horses now, and he guessed that Klein had stopped outside of town to plan the attack.

Jim ran down the alley to his house. He had almost forgotten Linda in the pressure of these moments. Perhaps she would be safe, but he would feel better if she were in the hotel. Besides, he needed every gun he could get, and Linda was worth two men at such a time. He reached his barn. The door was open and he saw that his roan was missing. He ran into the house, knowing that she was gone even before his search verified his suspicion.

Jim walked slowly back up the street, unable to believe that Linda had fled. It would have been like most women, but it was not like Linda Gale. He tried to think of some reason for it, to excuse her in his mind, but he could not.

Chapter Fifteen

When Jim came into the lobby from the back of the building, he saw that Doc Foster and Steele had piled mattresses against the front door and the windows.

"Leave the door open, Doc," Jim ordered.

"What the hell . . . ?" Foster sputtered.

"Do as I say."

Foster obeyed, grumbling sourly, and, when he had pulled the mattress back and opened the door, Jim stepped through it and stood on the boardwalk, listening. The racket of the fleeing townspeople had faded to the east; there was only silence now, the kind of silence that pulls a man's nerves out until he is almost crazy with the waiting.

Foster and Steele had taken their places at the windows, rifles shoved through cracks between the mattresses. It was fully light now, and for a time Jim thought that the storm was over and the sun was going to break through the clouds. Now he saw it would not. The sky had darkened again and a fine, cold rain filled the air.

Steele came to stand in the doorway

behind Jim. "I haven't seen them," he said, "but from the sound of their horses he must have an army."

"He's got his whole crew out there, I reckon," Jim said. "All but the men who belonged to Pruett. Funny thing about that. He never saw through Pruett's scheme."

"The man's an idiot," Steele snorted. "An egomaniac. That kind of a man is the easiest to fool there is."

"He's no idiot, no matter what else he is," Jim said. "I've got a hunch he let Angela get away so she'd warn us. He wanted the women and kids out of town, and he knew most of the men would leave if they had a chance."

Steele lit a cigar, nodding his agreement. "Sure, he's smart that way. He knows that, if this turned out to be a massacre, there'd be an investigation that'd ruin him. This way, people will think it was just a local range war, and Klein probably won't have any trouble. But I still say he's an egomaniac, or he'd have seen the way things were going."

Jim was silent, rolling a cigarette and smoking it while the minutes piled up. Then they came, a full twenty of them, shooting and yelling their intentions in bloodcurdling shouts, came with the thunder of eighty hoofs beating into the red mud of the street. Jim never knew what was in Klein's mind, but it was possible he had expected no real resistance. It was typical of K Cross, typical of Holt Klein who had ruled this country for so long, but it was a mistake and a fatal one.

Klein's men reached the business block before Jim cut loose with his first shot. Doc Foster and Steele began firing, and Dobe and Molly were shooting from their window upstairs. Smoke Malone, belly flat on the roof of the stable, let out a battle squall and got into the fight.

In that one instant everything changed. Three K Cross saddles were emptied; there was a turmoil of bucking horses and swirling gunsmoke and the agony cry of dying men. They fled on down the street, all but the three motionless bodies whose blood added to the red of the mud.

At the end of the block, Klein rallied his men and they reined in behind the buildings on the other side of the street. Within a matter of minutes they were crouching behind windows in the store and bank and Steele's office, their guns hammering out ragged volley after volley.

Jim and Steele wheeled inside the hotel as soon as the first wild rush had passed. They piled mattresses back against the door and moved to a window, their guns working with rhythmical precision.

"What do you think of them, making a rush like that?" Steele shouted above the thunder of guns.

"I think we fooled 'em. Klein didn't expect the reception we gave 'em."

"A more subtle man would have surrounded the town," Steele said, "but not Klein."

It was hot and furious for a time. Bullets sliced through the wall and sang across the lobby. They slapped into the desk, knocked the register half around, and sent the big ceiling lamp to swaying, coal oil pouring onto the floor until the lamp was empty. It was load and fire until guns were empty, and load again. Jim could not tell how much damage his side was doing, but there was no let-up in the crashing roar of guns from across the street.

"We've got all of Delaney's ammunition," Steele yelled, "but we can't keep this up!" He grabbed his shoulder and fell away from the window. "Damn them. I got tagged."

Foster dropped his Winchester and picked up his black bag. "I'll take a look."

"Keep your gun hot!" Steele shouted. "I'm all right."

"We can't afford to lose a man," Foster said. "Let me see."

Jim, looking around, saw Molly had come down the stairs and, dropping flat, crawled to where Foster was working on Steele. She said: "I've got a cut in my arm, Doc. Glass from the window, I think. Bleeding pretty bad anyhow."

"How's Dobe?" Jim asked.

"Shooting like he's crazy." Molly laughed. "You ought to see Angela. She's under the bed, carrying on like she was out of her mind."

"Probably she is," Jim said, and turned back to the window.

Suddenly, and for no apparent reason, Klein's bunch stopped firing. A moment later Dobe and Smoke Malone stopped. For a long time there was silence except for the thunder that had begun again.

"A trick," Steele said, crawling back to the window. "What will they gain by getting snaky now?"

"Dunno," Jim answered.

Molly returned to Dobe's room, and Foster picked up his gun and took his place at the window again. The minutes stretched out into an hour and then another, and still Jim could not guess what they were up to.

Suddenly Malone's gun cracked and he

let out a great squall. "Send another man, Klein! I just made a good Injun out of that one."

Steele laughed. "The damned fool would rather fight than be an engineer and do something useful."

"Klein must have sent a man around to the other side," Jim said worriedly. "The hell of it is we can't watch the street and the alley. If they get Malone, we're goners."

"I'll take a look," Foster said.

The doctor returned a few minutes later. "Couldn't see anything, Jim."

Again time ran out into what seemed an eternal ribbon. Steele said: "Past noon. I'm getting hungry."

"We won't do no eating for a while," Jim said. "They're probably full of crackers and cheese and figuring on waiting us out till we make a break."

Foster caught a hint of movement behind a store window and fired three times, fast. He grinned as he glanced at Jim. "I suppose that after while I'll have to patch up the holes I'm making."

Steele was sitting with his back to the mattress, long white hair matted and stained with blood. He lighted a cigar, shaking his head at Jim. "Doesn't look good, Sheriff. When it's dark, they'll close in."

"Might work two ways," Jim said. "When it's dark, I'll go after Klein."

"You wouldn't have a chance," Steele said bitterly.

It was raining hard now, big drops that slapped against the boards of the walk, and the air seemed to be filled with silver lances. A wind had sprung up, and the rain, slicing down from the Ramparts, splashed in through the broken windows and ran down the sides of the mattresses. Jim thought of his mother's suspicions about a storm being a conflict between the Lord and the devil. It was true now, the part about the devil anyhow, and again it was time to hold to the faith that moved mountains. Only a miracle would save them, but if there was enough faith, a miracle might be forthcoming, for faith was the material from which miracles were made. Crazy thinking, Jim told himself, the kind of thinking a man did when he had reached the end of his string.

"Bruce!"

Klein's voice cut into Jim's thoughts, bawling over the wail of the wind and the rattle of rain.

Jim shouted: "What do you want, Klein?"

"Waldron and Angela. Hand 'em over and we'll leave town."

It was a lie. Jim was sure of that, and when

he glanced at Steele, he saw that Steele had the same feeling.

"Tell him to go to hell," Foster said irritably. "He just wants to get us into the open and cut us down."

"No deal!" Jim called. "Waldron's in jail and he'll stay there."

Jim knew that it was a mistake the instant he said it. Waldron was locked up, unarmed and helpless. With this blinding curtain of rain drawn across the street, Klein's men could reach the jail without being seen distinctly enough to be shot down.

"Cover me," Jim said. He jerked the mattresses away from the door and opened it, ignoring Steele's and Foster's protesting yells. He lunged through the door, gun in hand, and ran toward the jail. Firing broke out again from the buildings across the street, but the rain gave him as much protection as it did the K Cross men who had rushed out of the bank.

Klein's riders raced through the mud toward the jail. Jim reached the jail before they did, the driving rain slapping into his face, drenching him and chilling him. He got a K Cross man in the belly with his first shot, then a slug caught him in the leg and knocked him down into the mud. Still, he kept his grip on his gun and, tilting it up, fired again and brought down a second man as a third lunged past him into the jail. It was Holt Klein.

Horsemen were in town then, sweeping in from the west, hoofs sending the red mud flying. There were yells and gunfire, and for an instant the street seemed choked, there were so many of them. More K Cross men had been in the street, but they were cut down under a hail of lead. Jim had no time to see who the newcomers were. Klein was inside the jail, and he had Waldron like he'd have a duck sitting in the middle of a pond.

Jim crawled to the door of the jail, dragging his injured leg, and pulled himself upright just as Klein's gun sounded. Then Klein, unaware that a new outfit had bought into the fight, swung back toward Jim, who stood in the doorway, a shoulder against the jamb.

They faced each other, unaware of the wind and the rain and the raging fight outside. They were aware only of each other, each knowing that the moment of final settlement had come. Pruett, Delaney, Waldron. Angela. All minor actors had been swept aside.

Here was a job Holt Klein could not give to anyone else. His heavy-jowled face showed that he understood. There was this one brief span of time when their eyes locked, when wills strained. The waiting was over. There was no talk in words, only the talk of guns.

Hammers dropped. Flames danced from gun muzzles, and the roar of .45s beat against the walls of Jim's office. Klein's bullet drove splinters from the jamb into the side of Jim's face; Jim's bullet drove life from the body of Holt Klein. He swayed, holding himself upright as he stared at the face of death. Then his gun dropped and he fell upon it, and his hat rolled and turned so that the crown pointed down.

Jim crawled toward the man, saw that he was dead, and went on to the door that led to the cells. George Waldron lay face down, motionless. Jim got back to the door. The rain had stopped, and he saw that it was the mesa bunch that had ridden in.

"Look at 'em run!" Howdy Gale crowed. "Who'd you think we was, Doc? Who'd ride like hell to buy into a fracas but the mesa bunch?"

Old Chinook was there. The younger Gale boys. The others who had watched the fight between Jim and Howdy that day that now seemed a long time ago. There were the girls Jim had seen the night Chinook had been saved from Sam Pruett's crew of hardcases.

Howdy saw Jim then and came toward him in long strides, mud squishing under his boots. "What the hell, Jim?" Howdy boomed. "Run into a buzz saw?"

Jim put a hand to his face and pulled it away, red with blood. "Sort of," he said, and pointed to Klein's body. "That's the end of it, Howdy."

Howdy peered past Jim and let out a howl that brought Steele and Doc Foster and Malone rushing toward the jail. "Take a look!" Howdy bawled. "Jim's got the old turkey laid out for stuffing."

There was a moment of silence as they looked and turned their eyes to Jim. Foster said slowly: "Well, it's over. Now I'll get at my job of patching."

Howdy and Malone helped Jim into the hotel lobby. Foster slashed Jim's pants' leg open and clucked at the wound as was his habit. "Not bad, Jim. But you'll have to take it easy. Reckon you can now."

"Not yet." Jim motioned to Malone. "Fetch Angela down here."

"No hurry," Steele said.

"Lots of hurry," Jim said. "This is the day. There'll be a dam on Wild Horse River and water in the valley. I'm going to see with my eyes what I've just been seeing in my mind. Go on, Malone."

Angela came, tearful and bedraggled. Jim, looking at her, felt some pity for her. Perhaps she deserved none, but he could not forget she had lived twelve years with Holt Klein. Any woman who had endured that had his pity. The law would not punish her, but now, staring at her tortured face, he thought that she would be punished through all the years of her life.

Dobe and Molly stood behind her, Molly's hand gripping Dobe's, and Jim saw that it was all right between them. Jim brought his gaze back to Angela's face. He said: "Holt's dead. That's what you've been wanting. It's what you wanted me to do, isn't it?"

"Yes," she said. "He was like a mad dog."

That was true, but Jim found himself thinking that perhaps Angela was the one who had made him mad. He said: "Pruett's dead. So's Delaney and Waldron. A lot more. You know why?"

"Yes. It was Holt. You know what he's done. . . ."

"And I'm thinking of what you've done."

She looked around, from Steele to Malone and on to the mesa people with their worn clothes and lean faces and lanky bodies honed down to bone and hide and muscle. She had no friends among them; she had no friends anywhere now.

"All right, Jim," she said in a tired voice. "You know what I've done. Are you going to hang me for Holt's crimes?"

"We won't hang you, but we're getting a new deal for everybody. The mesa people saved us and they saved the town. That means the rabbits who ran won't like it around here. We'll have a new banker and a new storekeeper. We'll have a dam on the river and a ditch system to put water on valley land . . . an honest system, Angela."

"And we'll have a few dams on the mesa," Malone added, "to hold back the spring run-off. Like on Lost Horse Creek."

"The hell you will!" Howdy Gale shouted angrily.

"Take it easy," Malone said. "You're done playing hermits. You'll have a school. A post office. You'll have water on mesa land. And you'll have law, or I don't judge Jim Bruce right."

Howdy struggled with his temper. It was Chinook who said: "We've seen it coming, Howdy, and now it's here. By damn, we'll help 'em build their dams."

The youngest Gale boy snickered. "By damn, we'll build dams."

Even Howdy laughed as he said: "Well, maybe we will have a new deal at that."

Jim's eyes were still pinned on Angela's face. He said: "Just one thing. K Cross goes to you like you figured it would when Holt cashed in."

"Only now it won't do me any good," she said in a low voice. "No crew. Everybody against me. That the way you want it, Jim?"

"No. I want you to sell to Colonel Steele. I think he'll make you a fair offer. Then you can take your money and go away."

She nodded, masking her face against the emotion that tore at her. "All right, Jim."

Jim motioned to Steele. "Take her to your office and make out the papers."

Nodding, Steele left the lobby. Angela hesitated, eyes searching Jim's face. She said softly: "It might have gone a different way, Jim, but you never believed me. You never believed me even when I told the truth." Then she followed Steele.

Later, when his splinter-speared face had been cleaned and bandaged and his leg wound attended to, Howdy helped Jim along the boardwalk to his house. Jim asked: "Where's Linda?"

"How would I know?" Howdy asked crossly. "She ain't our kin no more. I mean

. . . she left our house."

They turned up the path to Jim's place, Howdy holding his arm. Then they reached the porch and Jim looked up. Something hit him with the impact of a .45 slug. Linda, wearing a starched white dress and a red-checked apron, stood in the doorway, tall and straight, full red lips holding a smile that told him all he wanted to know. With bitter self-condemnation, he thought that he should have known she wouldn't run out on him.

"Damned fool woman," Howdy muttered. "Wouldn't come with us. After she fired the brush on Coyote Rock, she had to go home for that blasted dress."

"Help me up there!" Jim shouted. "What are you waiting on?"

Then he was beside her, and Howdy grunted: "Just mush and tush now. You don't need me no more."

Howdy swung around and strode off. Then, hanging to the doorjamb with one hand, Jim reached for Linda with the other, but she held back a moment, eyes on his bandaged face. She said: "You know what Angela told me, about not being fit for you." Her lips tightened. "But it isn't true. I was worried about it, but I'm not now. I want to be your wife, Jim, and live your way.

I just had to get this dress to show you how I looked."

"Sure," he said. "It's just like I knew it would be. You're the prettiest woman on Wild Horse River. Why, that ain't half big enough. You're the prettiest woman on the western slope. You're the. . . ."

"Hush, Jim." She blushed. "But I like to hear it."

He kissed her then, balanced on one leg, one hand still holding to the jamb. It was a new world, a good world, freshly washed by rain and warmed by the sun that was breaking through the clouds.

Jim Bruce had dreamed a dream, the kind that comes to few men. Now the road was cleared. The dream would become solid reality: sweet water carried in irrigation ditches to the thirsty valley, alfalfa fields would be emerald patches, and there would be good Hereford cattle to dot the valley, owned by many men. Holt Klein would be only a bad memory.

When Jim's term was up, Dobe could take the star and he'd be a good sheriff, with time. Jim would be back on Pitchfork, to live and let his roots go down into the rich soil, his and Linda's.

About the Author

Wayne D. Overholser won three Spur Awards from the Western Writers of America and has a long list of fine Western titles to his credit. He was born in Pomeroy, Washington, and attended the University of Montana, University of Oregon, and the University of Southern California before becoming a public schoolteacher and principal in various Oregon communities. He began writing for Western pulp magazines in 1936 and within a couple of years was a regular contributor to Street & Smith's *Western Story Magazine* and Fiction House's *Lariat Story Magazine*. *Buckaroo's Code* (1947) was his first Western novel and remains one of his best. In the 1950s and 1960s, having retired from academic work to concentrate on writing, he would publish as many as four books a year under his own name or a pseudonym, most prominently as Joseph Wayne. *The Violent Land* (1954), *The Lone Deputy* (1957), *The Bitter Night* (1961), and *Riders of the Sundowns* (1997) are among the finest of the Overholser titles. *The Sweet and Bitter Land* (1950), *Bunch Grass* (1955), and *Land of Promises* (1962) are among the best Joseph Wayne titles, and *Law Man* (1953) is a most rewarding novel under the pseudonym Lee Leighton. Overholser's Western novels, whatever the byline, are based on a solid knowledge of the history and customs of the 19th-Century West, particularly when set in his two favorite Western states, Oregon and Colorado. Many of his novels are first-person narratives, a technique that tends to bring an added dimension of vividness to the frontier experiences of his narrators and frequently, as in *Cast a Long Shadow* (1957), the female characters one encounters are among the most memorable. He wrote his numerous novels with a consistent skill and an uncommon sensitivity to the depths of human character. Almost invariably, his stories weave a spell of their own with their scenes and images of social and economic forces often in conflict and the diverse ways of life and personalities that made the American Western frontier so unique a time and place in human history.

We hope you have enjoyed this Large Print book. Other Thorndike, Wheeler or Chivers Press Large Print books are available at your library or directly from the publishers.

For more information about current and up-coming titles, please call or write, without obligation, to:

Publisher
Thorndike Press
295 Kennedy Memorial Drive
Waterville, ME   04901
Tel. (800) 223-1244

Or visit our Web site at:
www.gale.com/thorndike
www.gale.com/wheeler

OR

Chivers Large Print
published by BBC Audiobooks Ltd.
St James House, The Square
Lower Bristol Road
Bath BA2 3SB
England
Tel. +44(0) 800 136919
email: bbcaudiobooks@bbc.co.uk
www.bbcaudiobooks.co.uk

All our Large Print titles are designed for easy reading, and all our books are made to last.